# SURRENDER TO *Fire*

## LORA LEIGH

ELLORA'S CAVE
ROMANTICA PUBLISHING

# *What the critics are saying...*

so

## FYRE BRAND

**5 Angels and a Recommended Read** "I could go on and on about how well I enjoyed this book, but I am just going to highly recommend that anyone who enjoys erotic paranormal romance to pick this book up. Ms. Leigh is a master at her work and her talent fairly drips from every word." ~ *Fallen Angels Reviews*

## SURRENDER

**4.5 Stars** "This is a journey into the world of bondage and submission—and what a journey it is! More than a story about a woman submitting to a man, it's the story of a woman's discovery of the joy she receives at the hands of the man she loves. Leigh is an expert storyteller whose talent is not to be missed." ~ *Romantic Times Reviews*

An Ellora's Cave Romantica Publication

www.ellorascave.com

Surrender to Fire

ISBN 9781419959301
ALL RIGHTS RESERVED.
Fyre Brand Copyright © 2003 Lora Leigh
Surrender Copyright © 2003 Lora Leigh
Cover Art by Syneca.

This book printed in the U.S.A. by Jasmine–Jade Enterprises, LLC.

Electronic book Publication 2003, May 2009
Trade paperback Publication July 2009

# SURRENDER TO FIRE

ॐ

## FYRE BRAND
*~11~*

## SURRENDER
*~131~*

# FYRE BRAND
ৰ

# Dedication

❧

*To the wonderful ladies and family at EDBM. Pat, Barb, Tigg, Beth, Momma Sue, Stacey, Punque and Lue Anne. You encouraged me, supported me and nagged endlessly. You were friends when times were good and you held me up when times were bad. You always took time to explain what I didn't understand, and to read what you didn't always like. And through it all, you taught me to accept the stories that were a part of me. Thank you.*

# Prologue

ℰℴ

The files had finally arrived. Shannon Riedel, head of the Psychic Sensory Investigations Agency stared at the computer screen with a sense of resignation. The email cover letter said it all. File contained. Information, re: The Elementals. Executive clearance required.

"Computer, open file," she commanded softly.

"Executive level clearance passcode, please," the computer asked with its hollow monotone.

She typed in the first part of the code. "Pass code: Dream walker, seventh order, warrior rights. Zebra, seven of the sixth key." The oral passcode gave her level of clearance, the typed code gave a set of number and letters unique to her. The third key was her own unique voice, combined with the infrared eye scan that suddenly activated and her thumb scan from the small pad at the side of the flat keyboard.

She waited only seconds for the file to open. She felt her chest tighten in remorse when it did. Another death warrant, she wondered? There was nothing she hated worse than preparing evidence against a psychic. If they were psychic.

There were three young women rumored to be Elementals, the grandchildren of Tyre, a demon whose psychic abilities had nearly destroyed the world fifty years past. If these three women truly possessed Tyre's powers, then there wasn't a chance in hell she could save them. The Agency would demand their execution. Unless their powers could be neutralized by the PSI agents. Which was rare. Very rare.

She read through the information, frowning at the brevity of it, the lack of conclusive evidence. If the women held the most feared of psychic powers, then there was little evidence of it. The most damning fact was the evidence that Maile, daughter of the Tyrea, had claimed the girls as her granddaughters, though each child had carried different surnames. Different fathers? She rubbed at the tension settling in her brow.

Shannon sighed wearily. Psychics had once been a benefit to the world, now any good they could do was immediately reviled for the very power that could accomplish it. The horror of the psychic wars was too well remembered. Many cities within the U.S. were still rebuilding from the rubble that had been left in the wake of the final battle.

It was now Shannon's job, as director of the PSI agents, to evaluate the power the women held and make a determination of life or death to be passed to the Council. No mistakes could be made. She had risen among the ranks to take her seat as Director of the PSI Agency because she didn't make mistakes. And with these three women, her very life would be on the line. If she determined innocents should die, then her conscience would destroy her. But if she allowed such three powerful threats freedom, then the world could pay for her mistake.

She had to move carefully. If their powers could be controlled by the PSI agents, then there was a chance of saving their lives. But only a chance, and only if. She pushed her fingers through the short fall of her black hair and narrowed her eyes. It wasn't feasible to destroy them all. It wasn't humane.

As yet, there was no conclusive proof of psychic power, no reports of the women conspiring or socializing with known or suspected psychics. But, neither had they turned themselves in to the Psy-Guardians as the law required. A mark for them, a mark against them. She bit off a curse as she stared at their pictures once again. They didn't look like rebels or conspirators, but how many of that sort resembled the evil of their plans? Tyre had been one of the most handsome men known to be born. But his soul had been a cesspool of evil.

She drew in a deep breath. She needed more information. She couldn't condemn three women who had done nothing to warrant such extreme measure to death, without first being certain. She would have to send out three agents capable of learning this information for her. And of course, all restrictions on the ways they gained their knowledge must be lifted. There could be no doubts.

# Chapter One

๕ว

He touched her gently. Too gently. Carmella strained beneath Torren's tender strokes, forcing back the aggression rising inside her as her desire rose. His long, dark brown hair caressed her arms, creating a curtain of rough silk around his head while his tongue laved her hard nipple and his mouth suckled the eager point gently.

His hands, work-calloused and large, moved over her body with sensual knowledge, but with restraint. He was holding back, just as he always did. Her head tossed on the pillow as she bit her lip to keep from crying out in frustration.

"Adrenaline overload," he whispered against her breast, moving lower, his lips like a stroking flame over her skin. "Relax, Carmella."

His voice was thick and husky with lust as he nipped at the flesh of her abdomen, travelling closer to the center of the heat spreading through her body. But there was something more. A vein of knowledge she couldn't quite grasp...almost amusement. As though he knew the needs tormenting her and refused to ease them.

Her fingers clenched in the blankets of the bed beneath her as she fought for control. She could handle it, she assured herself, she always had before.

"Carmella." She opened her eyes, staring down at him as he paused over the pulsing mound of her cunt.

God, he was so rugged, so handsome. The angles of his face were an artist's dream. High cheekbones, the sharp slash of his nose, the stubborn chin. The male sensuality in the curve of his lips combined with the sun-darkened tone of his flesh gave him a brooding, intense look.

"Are you going to fuck me or talk to me all night?" She restrained the urge to bite him. Why did she always want to bite, to claw? The desperate throb of an almost violent lust surged through her veins.

Torren's lips quirked into a small smile. Too knowing. What knowledge did he possess that she didn't? And why couldn't she sift through the myriad psychic impulses to make sense of it?

"Eventually, I'll fuck you." His hand slid up her thigh, parting her legs further as the long strands of hair caressed her flesh.

Carmella shivered. She loved the feel of the silken strands on her skin.

"What do you mean, eventually?" She panted as she tried to tamp down the heated urges flowing through her.

She wanted to fight. Wanted to force him to restrain her, to plow inside her with every hard, throbbing inch of his thick cock. She trembled at the thought, allowing the image to flow through her mind as she whimpered in growing hunger.

"Damn, you're hot enough to burn me alive." His fingers skimmed the saturated curls between her thighs.

Her vagina pulsed, spilling the thick juices of her need from its gripping tunnel.

"Torren, stop teasing me." She wanted to scream, to demand that he give her the agonizing pleasure/pain her body was craving.

God, what was wrong with her? She needed him, loved him as she had never loved anyone. Torren fulfilled her. Soothed her. But nothing seemed to touch that dark core of lust growing steadily in her body.

Torren moved between her thighs, his eyes narrowed as he watched her. Hard, muscular legs spread hers; the broad head of his cock kissed the swollen lips of her pussy. Carmella shuddered, her hands fisting in the blankets as flames nearly erupted over her body. No. No. She couldn't let that happen.

She bit her lip, feeling the wide head of Torren's erection part the wet curves of her cunt. Her body was taut. She fought the flames and the agonizing pleasure as he began to stretch the delicate tissue of her vagina.

"Torren." Her strangled gasp was a plea. God, she couldn't be begging for something she knew she could never control. And she would never be able to stop her response to what she needed so desperately.

"It's okay, love." He sheltered her, coming over her as his hips worked his cock deeper insider her in smooth, shallow thrusts. "Hold onto me, Carmella," he whispered at her ear. "It's okay."

But it wasn't okay. The scream trapped in her throat was one of frustration and fury. The heat building through her body was too dangerous to ever relinquish control of.

"Hold onto me," he whispered again a second before his cock surged inside her, hard and deep.

She couldn't stop the keening cry that escaped. Couldn't halt the desperate spasm of her vagina around the thick, hot shaft impaling her. It was so good. Not what she needed, but so damned good.

His hair flowed around them, smelling of man and cleaning soap, damp and cool against her hot skin as he began to fuck her with a steady driving rhythm. Carmella arched her neck, her fingers tightening around the blankets gripped between them as dark lust surged through her body. Oh God. Her skin was heating, her blood flaming. Torren's cock stroked, caressed, tormenting sensitive, aching, nerve endings to a point of pleasure she could barely stand. She had to come soon. She had to.

"Now," she begged desperately as she fought the erupting power threatening to release. "Please, Torren. Please, now."

He slammed home. His arms tightened beneath her shoulders, his knees digging into the mattress as he began to fuck her hard and fast, pushing her close to the edge, so close...

Carmella couldn't contain her cry as the orgasm, lighter than she would have preferred, swept through her body, tightening it with pleasure. The desperate edge of hunger dulled as she heard Torren growl out his own release, the hot pulse of his semen emptying into her vagina as he tightened in her arms.

Breathing rough, her skin still prickling as heat raced beneath it, she tried to relax in his arms. She didn't want him to know how close to the edge she was coming. Couldn't face his realization of the perversions that tormented her.

"Okay now?" His lips caressed her cheek. A loving, gentle touch that brought tears to her eyes.

"Fine," she lied. She hated lying to him. Hated the needs that tormented her.

Torren moved to her side lazily, pulling her into his arms as he cuddled her close.

"Sleep, baby," he whispered. "Tomorrow's another day."

The reflective tone of his voice bothered her, but the fight to hold back the violence rising inside her took all her concentration now. She nodded against his chest, but she knew sleep would be a long time coming.

* * * * *

*We can't wait much longer.* Torren sent his thought to the man who waited miles from their location, pacing his rooms furiously.

*Dammit, Torren. I'm moving as fast as I can.* He could hear Ryder's lust pulsing in his voice. The connection he allowed the other man as he made love to Carmella had been strong. Ryder had sensed in every pore of his body the nearly uncontrolled needs sweeping through her.

Move faster, Torren suggested darkly. She nearly lost control tonight, Ryder. We can't afford to allow her to do that until you are with her.

A bleak pause followed his words.

Head to the beach house tomorrow. I'll have the Hummer waiting outside the east end of New Cincinnati. I'll cover her from here.

It was a risky plan. Torren stared down at Carmella, knowing she didn't sleep as she pretended to. Her muscles were taut, small goose bumps raised along her flesh as she fought the power coursing through her. He had to save her. He had to protect her. He kissed her head softly, enjoying the feel of her silken, fiery-colored hair against his lips.

She was a Fyrebrand. But even more than that, she was a blood link to the greatest psychic monster ever created. Her power was deep, strong. The psychic ability to spark and generate fire from thin air; to destroy, if need be, with flames hotter than any man could create, pulsed within her small body. And she was slowly losing control.

*I love her, Ryder.* But he knew and accepted that she would never be his alone. There was no jealousy, no anger in that thought. He had known for years that she belonged not just to him, but to Ryder as well.

*I'll take care of her, Torren.* The unspoken emotion lingered in Ryder's thought, as did the surge of dark, intense lust. He would complete the circle Carmella needed. He would complete them all.

Torren tightened his grip on her, holding her close, regretting the coming separation, but looking forward to the reunion. Carmella wasn't the only one restraining her lust, her darker desires. Torren was as well.

A smile crossed his lips. One he was glad Carmella couldn't see. Anticipation rolled through his body, thickening his cock, heating his blood. His hands smoothed over her back.

"You aren't asleep," he growled at her ear as he lifted her thigh over his, pushing his erection against the wet curves of her cunt.

Heat awaited him. A gripping, milking pleasure he needed one last time before he left her to Ryder's care. He rolled to his back, pulling her with him as she gasped in pleasure.

She impaled herself on the thick shaft, her back arching as she cried out at the pleasure he brought her. She surrounded him with fire, a lava-hot intensity he was more than willing to lose himself in.

"Ride me, Carmella." He gripped her hips as her small hands braced on his chest and she began to rise and fall along the hard length of flesh spearing into her. He gritted his teeth, his hips meeting her downward glide as he fought to take her easy, gently.

She cried out above him, her hips moving faster, harder, her pussy gripping him like a silken, slick fist. Torren gritted his teeth. His cock throbbed, ached to spew its hot release into the tight depths of her vagina.

His hands tightened on her hips, pushing her to ride him, to stroke the tight clasp of her pussy over his cock repeatedly. She was crying above him, her nails biting at the flesh of his chest, stroking his lust higher.

"Fuck me," he ordered her, his voice tight, nearly desperate. "All of me, Carmella."

He arched his hips, driving every hard inch inside her as she began to shudder convulsively, her cunt rippling along his shaft as her orgasm tightened her body. He thrust inside her again, hard, heavy, and then once more before he erupted inside her, groaning in pleasure, holding back the regret. It was much less than he wanted, but he knew soon—very soon—it would be everything the three of them needed.

# Chapter Two
## *Two Weeks Later*

ఆ

Carmella was wearing black. Ryder could only shake his head at this as he followed her in his astral form, staying between her and her pursuers, throwing the hounds off every chance he got and generally protecting the finely curved ass as it raced through the underbrush in the hills above New Cincinnati, Ohio.

She was dressed in the color of night from head to toe, form fitting, and snug. It was the color of mystery, of secrets. It was his color—and hers as well, it appeared. Her clothes hid nothing from his eager, astral gaze, though, and made his cock throb hard and demandingly in his physical body still sheltered in the inn back along the edges of town.

He kept up with her easily, drawing on Torren's added powers, as his astral form traveled farther away from his physical body than he was entirely comfortable with.

He sent her pursuers up and around the mountain with the false form of a young woman fleeing. As they moved, Carmella was forced to change her direction, opting instead for a path that led down the mountain to the safety of the inn she had been staying at in town.

She had gotten careless in her search for her commander and lover, Torren Graves, whom she believed had been captured by PSI, the Psychic Sensory Investigations unit of the new government, the week before. Her ties to Torren were strong, but her focus was faltering severely. If it weren't, she would have already been well aware of the fact that he wasn't in the prison she was watching so hard. She would have caught on instantly to the plan they had set in motion more than a month before. And the damned group of vigilantes would have never managed to surprise her as they had.

The coordination it had taken to draw everything together that night would terrify the director of the PSI if she ever realized he had managed to do it. There were things he kept from everyone, the true scope of his abilities being one of them.

The world wasn't ready to acknowledge that such powerful psychics were once again in the government.

He followed the woman, catching a glimpse of her expression as she glanced back at the lights that scoured the mountainside, a frown on her heart-shaped face as she realized the hounds had somehow lost her scent when they shouldn't have and were moving up the mountain, rather than on her heels.

He stilled his grin. She knew it wasn't logical. Carmella would never trust what wasn't logical. He had a hell of a fight ahead of him because his attraction for her, the rioting hunger that rose inside him, would never make sense to her.

He watched as those long, exquisite legs jumped a low boulder, her body hovering in the air for a long second before she hit the ground running again. Amazing. She twisted around the hulking forms of shadowed trees, avoiding more than one trap set to catch the unwary. She couldn't see them on the cloudless night, and he couldn't sense a flow of psychic power, though he knew he should have.

The power it would have taken to send out the "feelers" to detect the upcoming obstacles should have been near impossible for him to shield. Instead, he had only to worry about hiding her physical form. He should have been hard pressed to keep her safe. The fact that he wasn't had a twinge of excitement running through his veins. She was strong. Damned strong. It would make for a very interesting relationship.

*You have obstacles moving along the street at the point she'll enter.* Torren relayed the information to him telepathically.

Ryder could also feel his anticipation. He had been separated from Carmella for over a week now, giving Ryder time to accustom Carmella's unconscious mind to his presence, thereby assuring the conscious part of her that he could be worth the risk of trusting. Not that he expected it to be easy, though. Ryder sent a burst of power to the fleeing woman's left, giving the impression of a pursuer's light flickering in the underbrush. She shifted to the right, though he saw her hesitate. She was getting more suspicious now. She sensed no one there, saw only the light, and he knew she was starting to suspect she was being led along the path.

Carmella burst into the rubble-choked alley, bracing her hands on the concrete dune that stood in her way and flipping over it like an ethereal shadow. Then she stopped, hidden on the other side as he felt the tendrils of her power reaching out to him.

Avoiding them wasn't hard. She was trying to be cautious; to be certain there was no chance of touching the senses of the hounds still baying in the hills above her. But she also knew she was being watched.

Ryder shook his head and pulled back. He had her close enough to safety now and was fairly certain she would now find her own way to the Inn several blocks over. This had been his main objective, other than getting her ass away from the lynch mob that had detected her outside the prison grounds hours before.

I'm pulling back, he informed Torren. Cover my retreat.

The surge of power it took to return to his own body could be detected and tracked by another psychic, even one without astral power. He felt Torren providing the cover he needed as he forced himself to return from the astral plane and back to the physical.

Ryder opened his eyes the moment his psychic presence slammed back into the flesh and blood form. He drew in a deep breath as he fought the exhaustion that invariably came with such extreme use of his powers.

Ryder's lips quirked. He had been watching her for a week now as she searched the city for Torren. She was struggling with her own senses, the knowledge that her commander wasn't where she had been told he was. She was fighting herself so strongly that she refused to see the truth. Had refused to accept it even at the time Torren had offered it to her. The offer was rescinded now. Ryder would demand where Torren could not.

It wasn't going to be easy, leading her through her own fears, breaking her control. The grip she had on her own heightening desires was even tighter than the control she used psychically. Even more importantly, it was drawing away from the control she needed to focus and contain those powers.

Torren had been aware all along of Carmella's destiny. As a minor talent, his gift for seeing the potential of the future had been strong where Carmella and Ryder were concerned. He knew what had to be done, and he knew his part in it. The hard part would be convincing Carmella.

*She's on her way back in,* Torren informed him as he continued to follow Carmella. *She's suspicious.*

*We didn't expect it to be easy.* Ryder closed his eyes as he fought to still the anticipation of what was coming.

She's frightened, Ryder...

Bullshit, Ryder responded with an edge of amusement. She's pissed and she's getting careless. You aren't where you're supposed to be. She can't just kick ass and be done with it.

If there was one thing he had learned from Carmella's dreams, it was that the dominant, hard-edged side of her would cause complications in matters requiring a long degree of patience. She was quickly losing control rather than being able to wait and watch for the best opportunity to strike. It was going to get her killed.

*Yeah.* Torren's amused admiration of those qualities filtered through the mind connection easily. *That girl sure does look good kickin' ass, though, Ryder. It's a fine sight to see.*

Ryder snorted. Perhaps he would have seen it by now if his old buddy had been a bit more forthcoming when they had separated as a team years ago. Ryder had always wondered why Torren had sent him to join the group preparing to rebuild the government and the country, rather than both of them heading there.

The other man was an amazing tactician. As a seer, which was one of Torren's main psychic powers, he had the ability to glimpse what was coming and to know how to work toward it, or away from it. Rather than taking the job of working within that new government himself, though, he had sent Ryder.

PSI had been created to draw in those psychics with enough power to aid the rebuilding. It was also created to investigate and neutralize rebel psychics, and those intent on creating another demonic leadership such as Tyre's had been.

Carmella was under investigation not just because of the strength of her powers, but because of her connection to Tyre. The bloodline, which ran thick and strong, took her back to the two most powerful psychics the world had ever known—Tyre and the Tyrea.

That left her two choices now. She could submit to testing. If it was learned she could bond and be controlled by a disarming psychic whose only powers were that of neutralizing hers, or an absorber, who could soak it in, then she would live in relative peace. Or she could accept the drug the government had created that would control and eventually destroy her power. Otherwise, her freedom and possibly her life were at stake.

*We'll save her.* Torren's mental voice was as strong as Ryder's resolve.

*You should have told me sooner.* Ryder couldn't keep the edge of anger from his thought at the future Torren had not told him was coming.

Would you have left? Would you have done the work you have done? Would you have put in place the ties to this new government that will ultimately save her? Torren's questions were valid ones, and yet still that spark of jealousy remained.

Torren had found her, guided her, had been her lover for more than a year now while Ryder did the job he had been sent to do. During that time, his dreams had been in turmoil as his own lesser "seer" abilities had taunted him with her images while giving no clue to her whereabouts. Only after Torren had provided the necessary link had Ryder been able to slip into her unconscious mind and see the woman that had tormented him. A woman whose very life was now held in the balance of a government that was more than wary of any blood link back to the monster who had destroyed it once before.

The rewards will be worth it. Torren wasn't the least compassionate in his feelings toward Ryder's jealousy. Not that Ryder had expected him to be. I'll watch her while you sleep. Better get some rest, because she won't be as easy to conquer as you want to believe she will be.

Ryder didn't doubt that in the least.

# Chapter Three

ை

Carmella wasn't stupid. She knew she was being followed through her flight along the outer boundaries of New Cincinnati. She knew an astral watcher followed her, pushed her pursuers away from her and made a wide path of safety as she fought to escape the mob that had come upon her on the hill across from the prison.

Psychics were able to detect others of their kind, and were constantly on guard for them. But detecting those non-psychics, who had been taught to shield their thoughts, trained for years to hunt their fellow man and lived with the anticipation of the hunt, was harder. Especially when all her senses were concentrated elsewhere.

She needed Torren out of that prison — if he was there. She needed him out. She couldn't leave the area until she knew for certain he was safe. How the hell PSI had managed to capture him was a mystery to Carmella. She had known his obsession for that blonde-haired little witch of the new governor's would lead to nothing but trouble. But had he listened to her? Hell, no. Now there he was, drugged, trapped in the hellhole, unable to free himself or to help her free him. It was pissing her off. And it made no sense.

The blonde wasn't even his type. Delicate, fragile women had never appealed to him. Perhaps, it was Carmella's own jealousies that had her convinced of that. Her own pain as he had drawn away from her. He had been an anchor, a lifeline to the often tempestuous, nearly out-of-control emotions that could overtake her. He could draw her back with his passion, his gentleness. Even when she longed for something wilder, an intangible *something* she couldn't define or make sense of, Torren had eased her.

She moved quickly through the decades-old rubble and shadowed nightlife of New Cincinnati as she made her way back to the inn she was staying at. Finally, order was being established within the country. Lawlessness, lynch mobs and the desperation of a nation, she prayed, would slowly ease as the citizens replaced their nightly terrors with full stomachs and work-weary bodies.

Exhaustion clamored at her now. She was looking forward to a hot meal and the bed that awaited her. She moved carefully through the waste-filled alleys, making certain to stay within the shadows, to pull a close shield around the powerful abilities that could fairly hum with their strength if she wasn't careful.

Strangers were rare in the streets of New Cincinnati after dark. The lynch mobs knew who their locals were, made a point of it. Strangers were automatically distrusted, imprisoned, subjected to horrors she didn't want to relive for fear of never sleeping. She knew well the danger that awaited her if she was caught. It made the fact that she was being "watched" all the more worrisome.

She entered the torch-lit main room of the inn, ignoring the curious looks of the inhabitants as she stared around the bar. The inn had once been one of the many office buildings that sat outside the main thoroughfare of the city a century before. It was one of the few left standing.

The large central room held a multitude of tables and weary strangers to the city. Some she knew were psychics, some were bounty hunters, others were just killers.

She strode quickly through the long room, ignoring the distrustful, lecherous gazes of the men and the brooding, wary looks of the women as she made her way to a small, empty table in one corner.

She didn't like so many people watching her. The air felt thick with their emotions, the danger that surrounded many of them. It increased the nervous energy plaguing her now.

*You need to center yourself. Otherwise, a PSI spy will pick up on you instantly.* Torren's mental voice was cool, commanding.

*Where the fuck are you?* She was careful to keep her head lowered, her expression clear as he established the link that had been broken for over a week.

*I'm not really sure I can tell you.* There was a thread of amusement there that she knew she should worry about, but she was just too damned tired.

This isn't helping me any, Torren, she told him fiercely.

She was alone in this now. She was confident enough of her abilities to survive, but she missed Torren. Missed his support, his touch and the knowledge that there was someone to lean on.

*I'm sending someone to help you, Carmella.* His information had her holding her breath in surprise. *He'll be there soon. I want you to be waiting when he makes contact.*

There was something lingering in his thoughts that she couldn't quite put her finger on. Almost as though he didn't trust whomever he was sending.

*Oh, I trust him well enough.* There was a bit too much amusement in the thought.

*And he's supposed to help me how?* Irritation was crawling through her body. Dammit, she didn't like waiting around like this.

Stop, you're bleeding power! The command bordered on anger. Dammit, Carmella, you're losing control. Pull it in.

She tightened her jaw, doing just that. But it was damned hard. Her frustration level was becoming dangerously volatile.

You need to rest. I'm safe for now, he assured her. Get dinner, then fucking go to bed and sleep. You're too damned tired to keep stretching yourself like this.

And whose fault is that? She snarled silently, furiously. If you had kept your ass with me instead of sniffing some civilian honey pot I wouldn't be here now, would I, Torren?

It infuriated her. He was her lover, professed to love her, yet he had disappeared after nearly being caught trying to get close to the governor's daughter. A tempting, sensuous blonde who had drawn his gaze more than once during the speech the governor had given that day.

Sniffing some civilian honeypot? Mocking amusement accompanied Torren's thought. I never just sniff, Carmella. You should know that. Now be a good girl, stop being so jealous and get your dinner and some rest. You're wearing me down with all that frustration and weariness dragging at you. It's tiring.

Carmella clenched her teeth but refrained from growling as the waitress set a mug of beer in front of her.

"Dinner?" The slight woman's bored air pricked at Carmella's anger.

She glanced at the lighted menu display over the bar and sighed. It hadn't changed in days. Cabbage, potatoes, and boiled chicken with vegetables. Hell, it beat some meals she had been forced to eat.

"Dinner," she sighed, rubbing her brow. Torren was right; she was too damned tired for this.

The waitress nodded, moving away quickly as Carmella allowed her gaze to roam around the room in disinterest until the woman returned with her food. She ate quickly, efficiently. It was energy, nothing more, and as tired as she was she would need that energy just to pull her ass up the stairs to her room. As she pushed the plate back and picked up the mug of beer waiting beside it, she felt her senses hum in sudden awareness. She was being watched.

She could feel eyes on her, someone studying her, not astrally, but with such a physical presence it was disconcerting. The room was dim; especially the corners, but she found the offender easily enough.

Good God, he was a dangerous one. Carmella met his gaze for long seconds, her brow lifting mockingly as his look touched on her breasts pushing against the snug confines of her black top before meeting her gaze once again. His lips quirked in answering sarcasm.

He wasn't classically handsome. His features were too rough, too savage, for such a description. His thick, shoulder-length blond hair was pulled back from his forehead and restrained at the nape of his neck. Like her, he was dressed in black with a light leather overcoat that fell to his knees. Her eyes narrowed. The man was packing more than just muscle under that coat.

He was easily six two, with broad shoulders. She bet his stomach was flat and rippled with strength, his arms would be strong, his thighs powerful. Her vagina clenched at the thought. Staying power. He looked strong enough to have it, if he wanted it.

She sneered at herself. She hadn't met a man yet that could still the fires that raged in her body. It didn't keep her from aching, though. And the man watching her lit a flame in her womb that threatened to burn out of control. She could feel her body crackling with desire. Singeing with guilt. She was furious with Torren, yet was lusting after another man herself.

She pushed her fingers tiredly through her short red-gold hair, breaking away from his gaze quickly. Hell, she was so damned tired she knew she wasn't up to a fucking, no matter how good it could get, even if she was so inclined. But it didn't keep her from wanting.

Carmella pulled the price of her meal from her snug pants pocket as she rose to her feet and made her way to the second floor of the inn. The room she had taken had once been a small office suite. The entrance had a frayed, aging couch and single chair but was otherwise bare. It was the shower she needed right now, though. The dust and grime of a day spent hiding in trees and along the rough ground had done little for her disposition this evening.

Long minutes later she stood beneath the tepid, surprisingly fresh flow of water. This wasn't river water as she was used to. It was clean and sweet-smelling, with just a mild touch of chlorine. Evidently the city's water station was working ahead of schedule.

She didn't expect hot water, but was mildly surprised that even the chill had been knocked off it. She leaned against the rough shower wall, letting the lukewarm stream course over her after washing her hair and her body quickly, enjoying the rare pleasure of being totally clean.

The soothing spray of the water eased some of her tired muscles and relaxed her marginally. Minutes later, the rationed flow of water began to slow, and Carmella turned the taps off with a sigh of regret before stepping out of the shower stall.

With no more than a coarse towel wrapped around her body she moved through the central room and entered her bedroom.

She barely kept from betraying her awareness that she was being watched the moment she stepped into the room. It was the same presence that had followed her through the woods earlier, eerily similar to the sensation of the stranger's eyes that had watched her in the bar.

Who was he and what the hell did he want?

She had no doubt the presence was male. Who he was became the greater question, though. And why was he watching her?

# Chapter Four

ഇ

Carmella flipped the towel from her body, dropping it carelessly on the chair beside the bed as she feigned ignorance of the presence. She kept the shields around her own powers carefully in place, hiding her knowledge of the watcher as well as the strength of her psychic talents.

*Bad girl.* The amused chiding in Torren's voice at her display had her fighting a grin. *You always were a bit of an exhibitionist, weren't you, baby?* His arousal filled the connecting thought.

It surprised her, the dark undercurrents flowing through the connection. There was no jealousy, as she would have expected, only heat, approval. Arousal.

Naked, she moved to the bed, lying back on the soft mattress as she stared up at the ceiling.

Feels like the bastard from the bar earlier, she mused, knowing Torren was listening closely. He's powerful, whoever he is.

There was no answer forthcoming, as though he too were considering the uninvited visitor.

For a second, as her gaze had connected with the stranger, she had sensed a power in him, a hidden well of strength that aroused her curiosity and more.

He made you horny, Torren accused her with a thread of laughter. Be honest, Carmella, he made you wet.

She sent him the impression of her silent snort. It's not like you've been of any use to me lately. Too busy chasing after blonde bimbos.

Blonde bimbos can be a nice diversion. But I didn't fuck her, baby. I just wasn't fucking you.

She didn't like his tone, or the information. It hurt to realize his desire for her was fading. She hadn't expected that. But then again, she hadn't expected to be hit so quickly with her own lust for another man. She hastily censored her thoughts from the man who had been her lover, unwilling that he would know the innermost part of her longings. Longings she had never shared with anyone.

She had gotten close several times. Torren had nearly brought her to the release she needed once or twice when his fury with her had overwhelmed his consideration. But close didn't count except in battle.

The stranger at the bar had been powerful. Physically, at least, with a glimmer of carnal knowledge glowing in the blue eyes that had watched her across the room. Tall, strong, and if he was by chance psychic, then that physical power could be greater than normal. Enough to hold her down. Enough to thrust inside her with a strength and power that could ultimately push her over the edge. Maybe.

She sighed softly. She had never gone over the edge, so she had no idea what it would take to push her there. At five feet six, with a willowy slender body, she just didn't seem to inspire mindless lust in men. Torren seemed to want to protect her, rather than fuck her mindlessly. Not that the soft kisses and gentle touches weren't nice at times, but her sexual fantasies little resembled the touches she had received.

Her lips quirked. How surprised he would be to know the sexual fantasies that tormented her body. They were raw, carnal images that came from hearing the rough, sexually explicit descriptions of the acts she had overheard men talking of throughout her life. That and the words from the nearly ancient novels of another time.

She had found the cache of books years before in the hidden basement of a nearly demolished home. Paperbacks so close to falling apart she feared reading them. But once the words had leapt from the front page, she had been ensnared, helplessly caught. She had been as fascinated then as she was now with the excitement of being watched by a presence so strong it could slip past the psychic barriers she had placed around the room.

She had a job to do tomorrow. Wherever the hell Torren was hidden she had to find him so they could get the hell out of there before she was detected by the PSI agents that must surely be looking for her. But that was tomorrow and this was tonight.

Until then, she could play with her psychic Peeping Tom just a little bit. The surge of excitement at the thought of that sent the blood racing through her veins in excitement.

Watch me, she thought, thinking of the watcher as she opened her thoughts to Torren once again. Knowing her lover was "seeing" mentally what she was doing—feeling her arousal—brought a keen edge of excitement to her lust.

Damn. This is a dangerous game you're playing, little girl, he warned her, but his thought was filled with heated desire.

Enjoy it. She hid her grin from whoever watched. Let me enjoy it.

She closed her eyes, bringing to her mind the image of one of the rougher passages she had re-read not long before.

Her body was sizzling with lust, and though she could have slept while the watcher moved about the room, there was no way she could sleep with the fires of arousal burning in the depths of her pussy the way they were. She would give the bastard something to watch, to wonder about, and give herself the relief she needed to help her rest.

*Damn, Carmella.* Torren's curse was one of frustration rather than shock or disgust as the image filled her head.

She settled herself comfortably on the nearly flattened pillow, her hands rising to her already swollen breasts. She drew in a hard breath as her fingers smoothed over the distended peaks. Heat flared through her body, piercing her womb at the touch. She could feel her pussy creaming, soaking the red-gold curls between her thighs as she built the image of the written scene in her mind.

Her thumb and forefinger gripped her distended nipple, and she couldn't hold back a moan as she pinched it lightly. Then harder. Oh, that was good. Pleasure sang through her bloodstream, pounding through her body.

In her mind's eye it was the stranger from the bar touching her. Holding her captive against a wall, his powerful body blanketing hers, holding her still as she struggled to escape him. She would have to fight him. Fight to win. She didn't want a man she knew she could best; she wanted one strong enough to take her down and fuck her mindlessly even as she screamed out in fury.

*Fuck!* Torren's fierce, lascivious thought only made her hotter. He was seeing the image she was creating, images she had hidden before.

Torren had been uncomfortable during the few months he had been her lover, when he glimpsed the rioting needs that tormented her body. He was a strong alpha psychic, but he had no desire to assert the darker side of his passions. At least, not with her. She had a feeling the stranger who had watched her earlier would have no such problem.

She bit her lip, forcing back her moan of need as she twisted the hard point of her nipple. Her other hand smoothed over the flat plane of her stomach until it tucked between her thighs. She was wet; so slick and creamy her juices matted the curls that shielded her cunt.

She could feel Torren, still connected with her, watching her, his own arousal sizzling between them now in ways it had only threatened to before. But it was the stranger she saw. His hands touching her, tormenting her.

She imagined him holding her easily as she fought him, his hard body pressing her into the wall, his fingers twisting the tender flesh of her nipple as the fingers of his other hand took possession of her pussy. She arched away from the touch, but he followed her, his fingers sliding easily through the soaked slit to the clenching entrance below.

He wouldn't allow her satisfaction to come easily. She wouldn't submit to him without first testing him, pushing him past his own limits of control. And there lay her greatest desire...and her greatest fear.

He would have to take her control with the loss of his own. She didn't want a man able to maintain his own power, his own desires as she lost hers. She would want him to overpower her because he had no choice. Because his lust for her would be greater than his need to control his own power, physical or psychic. There were few psychics alive with the honor she required that would allow a lifetime of control to vanish for lust alone. But she could dream. And she could imagine such a thing occurring. And imagine she did.

\* \* \* \* \*

Ryder allowed his astral body to move closer to the bed, for the first time in his life afflicted with such lust, such overwhelming desire, that he could feel it even now, separated from his physical body. His psychic form felt every bit as sensitive, as heated as he would have been if he were physically standing by the bed watching her.

She was a hot little package. Her skin was smooth, creamy, with no betraying blemishes of disease or sickness. Her breasts were full, her stomach flat but by no means undernourished. Her legs were strong, rounded and slowly spreading to accommodate her slender hand as she caressed her wet cunt.

It wasn't the first time he had watched a woman masturbate, unaware he was in the room with her, but he'd be damned if it wasn't the most arousing. What was it about Carmella Dansford that tempted his control? And tempt it she did—in a number of ways that surprised Ryder.

As an alpha psychic, there was a part of him—a darkness he had kept hidden most of his life. It was one of the main reasons for the control he had built up over his lifetime. That darkness made him wary, and the desires it produced often made him wonder at his own sense of honor. Until now, no woman had ever strained that honor or the control he valued so highly. He was almost tempted to return to his physical body and wait until morning to contact her. That would have been the wisest course. But lust was never wise, and Ryder was filled with that blistering, foolish emotion in ways he never had been with another woman.

She was laid out before him, ripe and flushed, her breathing hard and deep as she pulled roughly at a hard, reddened nipple, while her fingers worked slowly through the swollen slit of her pussy. She was so fucking wet that the red-gold curls of her cunt glistened with the moisture that saturated them.

*Torren, son of a bitch, she's killing me.* It was only with the help of Torren's mental shield that he was able to hide his identity from her. He had no doubt she knew he was there.

The woman was a damned banquet of carnal delight. Her breasts would fit his hands perfectly, and he'd be damned if he didn't want to be the one twisting that perfect, hard nipple. He wouldn't allow her to smother her cries, though. He wanted to hear her screaming with the pleasure and erotic pain he could give her.

Her eyes were closed, her teeth clamped over her lower lip as she held back her cries. Her hips undulated against her fingers as she stroked the hot, wet flesh of her cunt. What was she thinking? What was she imagining? The need to know was driving him insane.

*Cover me. I'm going in,* he ordered Torren, unable to bear the thought that the other man was experiencing whatever fantasy she had conjured and that he alone was left to merely watch the results. He wanted to see the images filling her imagination—needed to know the key to Carmella's passions.

To do that, he would have to slip past the physical and enter her amazingly complicated mind.

*Damn, she might be more than either of us can handle, Ryder.* Torren's thought was a morass of lust, affection and anticipation.

He felt the added strength Torren sent to him as he stepped closer. Entering her mind undetected wouldn't be nearly as easy as entering her room had been. Her blocks were strong; her mind would be even stronger. But there was always a crack, a weak point. Ryder knew well there was no such thing as an impenetrable mind.

# Chapter Five

## ဢ

God help him. Ryder sent out the silent prayer after finding the weak spot in Carmella's defenses and slipping into the shadows of her daydream. She would be the death of him—and her, if he wasn't careful. Because when he got hold of her he was going to fuck her until he killed them both.

She was imagining him. It was the most amazing sight, seeing himself holding her against the wall, his hands rough, his hips pressed against that pretty ass as he held her in place. And she was fighting him tooth and nail. Fighting as her image of Torren wavered around them.

"Say no," the shadowy Ryder ordered. "When you say no, I'll let you go."

Ryder wondered if he actually got his hands on her, if he could let her go should she actually say no.

"Go to hell." Her curse echoed in the confines of the dream she had built within her mind.

"Wrong answer," the dream Ryder taunted.

His hand moved from between her thighs to deliver a stinging slap to the well-rounded curve of her buttock. Ryder watched her flinch, heard her cry out. Son of a bitch, it was her daydream and it couldn't have hit his own fantasies much closer.

He watched as she struggled, kicking back, her head tossing as she tried to slam it into her dream lover's face. The male vision only chuckled, then smacked her again a second before his fingers delved into the cleft of her ass and slid to the area of her pussy.

It was wet. Ryder knew she was dripping wet without seeing it. The dream Ryder hummed his appreciation of what he found as the woman bucked in his arms.

He forced her legs apart then, his powerful thighs flexing. She screamed in outrage, cursing him as his body bent, his cock lining up between her thighs. Ryder had a second to glimpse the penetration of her cunt.

He stood back, watching as the pair fucked furiously. The dream Ryder was hard-pressed to keep his cock inside her as she fought him, but somehow he managed. She tossed and writhed, then whimpered as she came. The orgasm was light, her body pulsing for more. Behind her, her lover stiffened, driving his erection inside her one last time as he obviously spent himself as well.

She was nowhere near satisfied, despite her orgasm. She needed more, yet seemed too tired, too frustrated to bring herself to peak once more. He hid in the shadows of her mind as he felt the exhaustion sweeping over her. Sleep would come soon.

He had slipped into her mind while she was occupied with her own needs, but her subconscious would be used to him now.

Her mind darkened—images, memories, flickering about the mists that began to fill her subconscious. He stood back, waiting, knowing that when sleep took over another part of her would awaken. It was this part of her he longed to see.

The little fantasy he had glimpsed had intrigued him, giving him more than one clue into Carmella's sexuality. But he needed more. He didn't expect what came to him.

He saw the pages of a book, then the images jumping to life on the tapestry of her subconscious. He watched in surprise and lust at the twisting figures that began to fill her mind. In each, the female was in a position of submission, two males, out of control and consumed with lust, filling her. He was going to explode with his own arousal, Ryder thought heatedly. The female images were Carmella, the males' misty forms were his and Torren's. And they were willing to force her compliance. She was starving for raw, carnal sex. To submit, to be taken. Not raped, but forced to relinquish her own control to a man—or men—strong enough to take it. Someone stronger, more powerful than she.

She fought in each sequence of events. Struggled against the males' greater strength only to eventually accept the spears of hard, eager cocks ready to take her. But even in the midst of the lust, he saw something more. In each one Carmella's dream lovers, though out of control, never truly hurt her. The voices were rough, though tender; commanding, but not unkind. And after possessing whichever part of her body one of the shadowed shapes managed to penetrate, they praised her.

The tight fit of her small pussy, the heat of her ass, the grip of her mouth or the stroke of her tongue—each image, each fantasy, was different. And here was the key to the woman.

He eased back from her then, aware he was close to the edge of his own control and moving closer toward the vilest act a psychic could participate in. Taking her in this vulnerable time of her greatest need. And he could. He could weave his astral force into one of the shadowed male shapes and give her what she fantasized about. Without her consent. Without her own conscious realization that it was, indeed, what she wanted.

He forced himself through the small break in her barrier that he had found. He repaired it quickly, reinforced it to keep her safe then returned to his own body.

Ryder sighed deeply as he looked away. He stared up at the ceiling, contemplating his options. He liked to consider himself practical—kind in many respects. He worked for the new government because he knew the laws being put in place were for the protection of everyone—psychics and non-psychics alike. Laws that would be set up as unbreakable for the protection of everyone. Laws that, if in place now, would assure his instant punishment.

*She won't be easy,* he told Torren, amazed at the sense of gentleness he was suddenly feeling toward her.

She knew I was there when she took that little fantasy trip. She's strong. She's losing her defenses. Torren's tone was concerned. She's too tired.

*Can you shield her until she awakens?* That could be a complication. If she were that tired, then her powers would be easily detected by the PSI searching for emanations of psychic strength that weren't contained by the government-issued restrainers created for civilian psychics, or the unique signal of a tested PSI member.

*As always.* Torren's softer emotions for the girl filled his thoughts. He was worried, aroused, eager. But her protection was uppermost. As it always had been, even before she had come into Torren's life.

Ryder shook his head as he remembered his first contact with Torren right before receiving the file on Carmella from the PSI director. The future he had predicted had made little sense until he received the file and saw the woman who had occupied his fantasies for years. The same woman PSI was now contemplating extreme measures against because of her link to the past.

Fyrebrands were elemental psychics. The creation of that particular psychic talent had been artificial. Tyre had been extremely adept in the elemental powers, as had his wife, the Tyrea. They had been the most powerful and had easily taken positions of leadership. Since then, every advanced elemental discovered had been found to trace back to Tyre. The man had impregnated more women than those recording it at the time could keep track of. But his mate had been Leila, the Tyrea. The birth of her daughter had been discovered, as had the efforts taken to hide her as the war had started to turn the tide in favor of those fighting to destroy the merciless psychics who had taken power.

Where the child had gone wasn't learned until after her death. But it was reported that she, too, had given birth. That direct bloodline of the two most powerful psychics was suspected to run in Carmella's veins. If it did, then her life hung in the balance if it was ever discovered.

# Chapter Six

## ഇ

The next evening the stranger returned. Carmella watched as he entered the inn, his gaze catching hers immediately as he stopped at the bar once again.

*Who is he?* She knew Torren was in her mind, watching her, keeping track of her movements, but he hadn't yet offered to reveal his location.

She hadn't even bothered returning to the prison. She knew she wouldn't find him there. Whatever game he was playing would have to be endured until he was satisfied. She had learned that a long time ago. It didn't mean she had to like it.

The day had been a fucking washout, Carmella thought as she sat with the back of her chair braced against the wall. She had scoured the city, wondering where Torren was, and having nothing but the conversations he kept up in her head to go by. But she never sensed a strengthening in the mental link. She was starting to think he was nowhere near the city.

She glanced broodingly at the stranger who made no effort to hide his interest in her. She finished off the shot of whisky she had ordered after her meal, refusing to redirect her gaze.

Her dreams the night before had been filled with him. Stark, vivid, lust-filled dreams that left her aching, her pussy wet, her breasts sensitive. She had never had such a reaction to a man. Had never been so certain that one could stem the rising fury of need that sometimes grew inside her, tormenting her body and her mind before she found a way to push it back.

Several times throughout the day she had been forced to tamp down the overriding lust. It grew in her, like a shadow of fury that threatened to rage out of control.

She rolled the small shot glass on its end, her fingers gripping it lightly as her gaze returned to the blond-haired, blue-eyed temptation that stalked her dreams, and now her evenings. Why was he just watching her? If he was Torren's friend, why hadn't he made contact yet?

I'm sure he'll let you know eventually. Amusement whispered through her mind.

*Is he the one you contacted?* She knew Torren could easily detect her anger. It grated on her that he refused to tell her where he was, yet trusted another instead.

*And if I don't know where I am?* he asked her, his voice silky, almost...deceptive. And he didn't say if he knew the guy or not.

I won't know if it's him until he gives you the information I gave him.

She sighed tiredly. Why am I getting the feeling you're setting me up, Torren?

She couldn't ignore it any longer. He wasn't where he was supposed to be. His telepathy wasn't cut off. If PSI had him, he wouldn't have a chance of linking with her mentally. Which meant PSI didn't have him. But neither was he helping her find him. Her frustration level, high to begin with, was only growing daily.

*Have I ever hurt you, Carmella?* She couldn't ignore the affection he felt for her. The truth of his loyalty to her. It was all there. Just as it had always been.

*No.* She pushed her fingers restlessly through her hair, glancing back at the stranger.

I won't start now.

Torren wouldn't, but what about the stranger? She had to do something soon. She was becoming too frustrated, too near to losing her control. And this unknown man wasn't helping. He made her hot. Too damned hot and in all the wrong ways.

Carmella sighed tiredly. Her temper was fraying at the edges. Ever since the first glimpse of that man the night before, she had been tormented with images of him rising over her, taking her, his hard cock driving into her repeatedly. The muscles of her cunt clenched as she fought to pull her thoughts back.

His lips quirked in wicked humor, a dark blond brow arching faintly in question as his gaze stayed on hers. Damn, he looked too sexy—too male. And clean. Son of a bitch if the man didn't look clean. There were few in the bar that could claim that distinction, even herself.

The stranger was dressed completely in black. Black boots, jeans, shirt and leather overcoat. He looked as tough as rawhide and too tempting for his own good.

The dark clothing seemed to only further accentuate his almost white-blond hair and wicked blue eyes. His dark skin, the sardonic quirk of his lips, the well-trimmed dark gold beard and mustache all combined to make him look like a pirate. A marauder. A sexy, untamed male.

She kept her gaze on him as she stood up from her chair and began to work her way to the bar, ignoring the heated pace of her heartbeat that seemed to echo in the depths of her pussy. What was it about this man—a stranger—that affected her as no other had?

She moved through the crowded room, ignoring murmured invitations from various men as she passed, keeping her gaze on the stranger until she slid between him and the bar stool beside him.

Neither budged. Her breasts were pressed tightly against his chest as he stared down at her broodingly, the heat of his body whipping through her nipples where they pressed against the cool expanse of his leather overcoat.

"Bartender, whisky," she gave her order as she fought to keep from panting.

As the bartender moved to fill the order she felt a wide palm at her hip. It was steady, moving no further, cupping the curve of her body with a heated caress. She raised her eyes to him.

"Who the fuck are you?" she hissed low enough that only he heard her words.

She felt like ramming her knee into the intriguing bulge between his thighs when his sensual lips tilted in a mocking smile, his hooded eyes glimmering with lustful purpose.

His head lowered, moving next to hers, his lips whispering against the sensitive lobe of her ear as he whispered, "Your most erotic fantasy." His voice was dark, deep, a sensual rasp over her senses that sent her clit throbbing, her heart pounding. "Are you going to say no?"

Carmella's eyes widened as the memory of her fantasy the night before surged through her mind.

*Say no and I'll let you go.* It was her fantasy. Or was it?

He moved back slowly, his expression erotically intense, his lips parted just enough to make the sensual male curve a temptation she could barely deny. At her hip, his fingers flexed, stroked, his fingertips inching beneath the snug hem of her shirt at the waistband of her pants.

She flinched at the stroke of pure sensation as his fingertips smoothed against her bare flesh. Calloused. Warm. Creating an erogenous zone where none should exist.

Psychic. She knew he was, but she couldn't sense any emanations of power at all. Carmella had a sensitive awareness for those psychic waves, yet she could detect nothing.

"I'll do better than that," she whispered at his ear, licking her lips, allowing the tip of her tongue to barely glance the strong line of his earlobe. "If you want it, big boy, you have to take it. Think you can?"

Before he could reply she collected her shot glass, threw back the hard liquor and moved away from him. She glanced back to see him watching her, his head lowered, his gaze brooding. The look sent an arc of pure arousal pulsing through her body and a sudden, overriding image of him doing just as she had dared him to do.

*Oh, bad girl.* Torren was laughing at her as she swept from the room. *A challenge like that would be hard for a man to refuse. You just gave him permission to force you, Carmella.*

*Only if he's man enough.* She hadn't yet found a man who could overpower her. Psychic or not.

Torren was quiet for long, intense moments.

*You might get more than you bargained for.* His thought was heavy with warning, and a small, thrilling spark of lust she had always felt he kept carefully hidden.

*You had your chance.* She threw the door open to the small suite of rooms. *You wanted a bimbo, honey, instead.*

The door bounced on the inner wall then swung forward again. Carmella caught it and slammed it closed before clenching her fists and fighting for control. She could feel the anger, the throttled desire and frustration building inside her. She needed a good fight but there was none available. No, she needed a good fight and a hard fuck. She trembled at the thought, the muscles of her pussy rippling.

"Where are you?" she growled as she stalked to the dingy window of the room, looking out into the darkened street with a sense of helpless rage. "I'm tired of this game, Torren." The sound of her own voice was a comfort for her, even though it wasn't needed for him to hear her.

*If only it were a game, Carmella.* His lingering regret washed through, and a frown creased her brow as she felt it. *I wish it were no more than a game. Then you would find ease and I would find peace.*

She laid her head against the pane of glass, ignoring her reflection as well as the regret that lay heavy in her heart.

Yeah, she agreed silently. If only it were a game.

# Chapter Seven

**ഉ**

The knock came on the main door to the suite the next morning, just after a quick breakfast of bacon and toast purchased from the restaurant downstairs. She came to her feet slowly, sending out a cautious mental feeler for any signs of aggression outside the wood panel.

She sensed Torren then, slipping into her mind, watching cautiously.

Can you tell who it is? she asked suspiciously.

I don't feel danger. No sign of aggression. The knock came again.

Gripping the heavy blaster pistol strapped to her side, she moved slowly to the door. She lifted the long weapon from its holster, keeping it at shoulder level as she quickly turned the door knob and threw it open. She moved to the side of the frame and brought the weapon to bear on a more than impressive chest.

She breathed out deeply as she stared at the visitor smirking down at her.

"What the fuck do you want?" The instant antagonism was followed by a hard pulse of moisture between her thighs.

Without waiting for an invitation, he placed his hand on the door and pushed past her, stepping into the room.

The aggressive arrogant move had her forcibly tamping down the power that sparked inside her. She could feel her stomach tightening, heat flaring in the depths of it. He lifted a brow mockingly as he passed her.

She quickly holstered the blaster as she moved back into the room, slamming the door behind her. Fury surged hard and fast through her veins as she fought the overwhelming response as the man turned to face her.

Her senses were going crazy, impressions tumbling in on her, a confused jumble of fear and knowledge. And danger. She could feel it licking over her flesh like a lover's caress.

This is your doing, she accused Torren furiously. I know this is your doing. You can't hide it, you son of a bitch. What are you up to?

*You don't know any such thing. Settle down, Carmella. See what he wants.* Torren's demanding presence did little to still the sudden confusion running rife through her.

Her eyes narrowed on the stranger as his gaze flickered to her heaving breasts beneath the snug fit of her black top. Her nipples peaked, and her senses fractured beneath the lust in his eyes when they rose back to hers.

"I would think what I want would be obvious by now." His blue eyes were sparkling with laughter as he watched her.

Carmella snarled. Arrogance strengthened every line of his face and glittered in his eyes.

"Well, let's pretend it's not," she suggested sarcastically. "Who the hell are you and what are you doing stalking me?"

He crossed his arms over the black shirt he wore, causing the material to stretch over the bulging muscles of his arms. Strong, thick muscles. She gave herself a mental shake as she felt Torren's amusement.

If this is your little buddy, Torren, I'll roast you when I find you, she promised him silently.

"I imagine Torren's been in contact with you by now," the stranger suggested softly. "He sent me to bring you to him. I'm Ryder."

Carmella stilled. He didn't say Torren had sent him to help her find him, but to take her to him.

Torren? Does he know where you are?

It's possible. She could hear the mental shrug in his voice. If it's really Ryder, then anything is possible.

*And how the hell am I supposed to know?* She watched the other man carefully as she mentally thought of all the ways she could kill Torren. Slowly.

Ryder watched her mockingly as she fought for answers, his demon's blue eyes tracking each curve of her body until he returned to her face. When he saw her gaze, a confident, sensual smile crossed his expression. She could see the male superiority in his gaze, the complete assurance that she would do as he wanted.

The aggressive arrogance in his attitude had her forcibly tamping down the power that sparked inside her. She could feel her stomach tightening, heat flaring in the depths of it. He lifted a brow mockingly.

*Carmella.* Torren's warning thought drew her attention from the other man. *You're bleeding power again. Rein it in.*

She breathed in deeply. The amount of psychic static her powers generated would bring any and every PSI agent within a ten-mile radius running if she weren't careful.

"My shield covers you," Ryder told her as his lips quirked in amusement. "Go ahead and get mad. I'm sure I can handle it."

He wore arrogant superiority as easily as he wore the faded black jeans. His voice resonated with it, sparking something inside her that she tried to convince herself was anger alone. But she knew better. And she knew Torren would as well.

Son of a bitch, she didn't need her lover trampling through her mind right now. It was strange as hell to lust after another man while the man she had fucked more than once looked on. But it was also discomfortingly arousing. It added an edge she didn't want to look deeply into.

"And how the hell am I supposed to be sure Torren even knows you?" She propped her hands on her hips as she watched him distrustfully.

"Because I just said he did." He shrugged his wide shoulders, his arms still crossed over his muscular chest as he watched her, almost laughing at her.

"Oh, and I'm just going to accept that," she assured him, thickening the mockery in her voice. "I don't think so, big boy."

He chuckled, a low, rough sound that caused her cunt to clench heatedly.

"Torren told you I was coming, Carmella. He's with you now. The code was simply Ryder. Or, ride her. I rather liked the idea of the latter."

*You didn't,* she hissed silently, furiously.

*Oh come on, Carmella, I'm sure he misunderstood.* But she heard the laughter in his voice. The knowledge that he most likely had done just that.

Ride her! She hoped her snarl conveyed itself across the mental channel. Ride her! I should let him while you watch, you sick bastard.

The surge of lust that speared her mind shocked her. The thought of it aroused him almost as much as it did her.

"I don't know you, and Torren never mentioned you to me," she assured him softly as her hand lowered to palm the butt of the pistol. "Try again. Get the code right this time."

"You didn't have a code with Torren, but you slept with him," he growled, a glimmer of possessive anger sparkling in his gaze. "Now you'll sleep with me."

*Damn, he sounds kinda pissed over it.* Carmella ignored Torren's amusement at the other man as she stilled. She belonged to no one but herself, yet this man acted as though he had somehow claimed her for his own. A claiming she had no say in. She didn't think so.

"Torren doesn't acknowledge you," she informed him softly. "And you have no rights to me. Period."

"Yes, he has acknowledged me." His eyes narrowed on her expression. "As a matter of fact, he's rather amused right now, I believe."

"Prove it," she challenged him, her senses flaring, anticipation spreading through her body. She could force the fight she needed so damned bad, then she could talk reasonably. She would show him first, though, that she wouldn't be mocked. She wouldn't be ordered. Not unless he could do what no man had before.

"I can give you what he couldn't, Carmella," he told her softly. "I can make you submit."

Her eyes widened as she felt her face pale. "I don't know what you're talking about."

"Don't you?" he asked her softly. "I think you do, baby. And I think you're dying to find out if I can."

You expect me to just follow this bastard? she snorted silently to Torren. What does he do, buy his arrogance wholesale?

Torren's answering amusement wasn't much help.

Carmella watched Ryder as she stilled the pulse of arousal and fury churning through her system. Emotion only clouded her mind, and as desperately as she needed to find Torren, she would be damned if she would just accept and follow anyone.

Unfortunately, Torren was doing little to help her. He was neither agreeing nor disagreeing with anything Ryder was saying. His amusement whispered through her mind, as though he enjoyed the confrontation playing out before him.

"And I think you're a bit too damned arrogant," she growled. "I want to find Torren, not fuck." She forced the lie through her teeth as she faced him. "You aren't saying anything to convince me you can help me with that."

"That's your pride talking," he said softly. "You already know Torren sent me. And trust me, I can find him. But not without boundaries. I lead. You follow. It's that simple."

Nothing was that simple. Carmella could sense the hidden currents flowing from him, the dominance that was as much a part of him as the blue of his eyes, or the brilliant white of his hair.

She breathed in deeply, fighting for patience as she stared across the room at him. He was too forceful. Too dominating. She could feel her body tensing, the urge to fight swelling within her. He made her want things she knew would never truly exist, and it terrified her.

She pushed her fingers restlessly through her hair as she fought to think logically. Okay, Torren had sent him...

I wouldn't send anyone that couldn't do the job right, Carmella. His thought was suddenly strong, pulsing. He's saying all the right words, but I don't know for sure.

His suddenly cool demeanor worried her.

Then how the hell am I supposed to know? she snapped silently.

There was no answer forthcoming.

"Standing here looking at you isn't a hardship, but it's not getting us any closer to Torren either," Ryder smirked. "Are you ready to ride or not?"

The blatant sexuality of the question had her hackles rising instantly.

"Excuse me?" She could feel her power pulsing, energizing.

The grin that tilted his lips did little to ease her mind. It was pure sexuality, unapologetic, richly sensual.

"I'm ready to leave now. Get your things and let's go."

He expected her to just follow him? To mindlessly accept that he could be trusted?

"I don't think so." She braced her body, watching him carefully. "I don't just follow anyone, Ryder. Not even on Torren's command. Which he hasn't given me, by the way. It's not going to be that easy."

*Challenge?* she asked Torren.

There was a long, thoughtful silence. *It's the only way to know for sure. I know how he fights. But the challenge you put out last night might get you more than you're bargaining for.*

Her responses leaped in a betraying surge of arousal at the thought. She smiled slowly, watching Ryder's gaze darken at the movement.

"Torren's a smart bastard." She shrugged her shoulders negligently. "But I'm not exactly stupid. You haven't yet proved you can lead and until you do, you'll have no loyalty from me." He was cocky enough, Carmella gave him that. If arrogance and superiority equaled strength, then he'd have it licked. But they didn't. They often equaled a too-large ego and too little power.

Carmella smirked in Ryder's direction.

His gaze became hooded, sweeping slowly over her body as she stood facing him. She kept her body loose, prepared to jump. She wouldn't let him surprise her.

"Who said anything about wanting your loyalty?" he murmured, the blue of his eyes deepening. "The strongest rules *and* rides. Are you sure you can handle that?" The sexual connotations had her brow rising slowly.

Her lips quirked at the challenge. "Think you're man enough?"

"Oh baby." He grinned then, and there was no hiding the heat of lust that flared in his gaze. "I know I am."

# Chapter Eight

## ஐ

Overconfidence had been many a man's downfall when it came to her, Carmella assured herself. She had faced off against more than one, and only Torren had ever beaten her. And even then, Carmella felt it was closer to a draw than an actual loss on her side.

As she placed her pistol and assorted knives out of the way, her eyes narrowed on him. Balancing herself carefully, she allowed the shields around her powers to drop. She felt Torren reaching out across whatever distance separated them, his own power shielding the room, covering them from PSI detection.

Instantly the room hummed, crackling with energy as the force of her elemental power began to grow within her. She would fight him with everything she had and she would show him who would rule and who would ride. She snorted silently, watching him carefully as he flexed the powerful muscles beneath his shirt and watched her with a smug quirk to his lips.

"I'm giving you one chance, Carmella," he said softly. "We can do this the easy way."

"Can you tell me where Torren is located?" she demanded as she let her arms rest at her sides, her fingers flexing as energy traveled through them.

He sighed, shaking his head mockingly. "Sorry."

She shrugged in return, allowing a smile to tilt her lips. "Then I guess we'll have to fight it out, won't we?"

"Carmella, if I take you down I'll fuck you." He almost shocked her with his explicit words. "It won't be nice, or easy, and it sure as hell won't be the least bit romantic. I'll plow as deep inside your pussy as I can. And it won't stop there."

Carmella tried to still the surge of lust that swept through her womb. She had never been taken down, dominated, fucked until she screamed. She had fantasized about it. Had dreamed of it. But it had never happened. She shook her head slowly.

*Well, he's confident anyway.* Torren's thought was too amused to suit her.

Shut up and let me concentrate, she told him absently.

*With a threat like that you'll lose for the hell of it,* Torren quipped as Carmella tried to push him from her mind.

"Promises, promises," she sighed mockingly as his gaze flickered to the beaded tips of her nipples beneath her snug top. "You're such a tease, Ryder."

Ryder chuckled softly as his gaze returned to hers. "Taking you down will be a pleasure, Carmella."

She licked her lips slowly, sensually. "Are you going to talk me to death, big boy, or actually make a move?"

He made his move with a speed she didn't expect, leaping for her in an effort to enclose her in his arms.

He was fast. She had to give him credit for it. And, son of a bitch, if he wasn't powerful. Static filled the room, flipping around her as she spun out of reach, ducking and twisting to the side as he grasped for her. At the last minute, she extended her leg in a kick that had him cursing as it glanced his shin. Power filled her.

He hadn't come at her with a psychic blow, but depended on physical strength instead. As she flipped around to face him she sent a surge of static in his direction. Crackling mid-air like an invisible whip, the arc of energy should have struck him across his chest, putting him down for several long moments.

Instead it fizzled out against an invisible barrier inches from his body. Her eyes narrowed. Someone had to be providing Ryder with his own amplifying powers. "Call off the guard dog," she snarled. "Fight me alone or don't fight me at all."

"Did I say I was going to play fair, Carmella?" he asked her gently as he glided around to the other side of the room. "Your powers are elemental. Fire, if I remember correctly, with a few lesser talents thrown in. Do you think I'd drop my guard?"

She lifted her lip in a sneer. Anger surged through her, but the lust pounded just beneath her skin.

"You aren't defenseless," she accused him softly as she worked her way to the center of the room, watching him carefully.

"Neither are you, baby." He grinned. "Come on, Carmella, burn me. I dare you."

She laughed softly. "Come and get me, Ryder." She spread her arms wide. "If you can."

She sensed the attack coming. A whip of dead space. It nearly terrified her. She dropped to the floor, sending a surge of fire in the direction it came from as she processed immediately whether to jump or roll. She jumped, clearing the disarming shock with less than an inch to spare as she threw a blast of deadly flames at Ryder's head.

She heard him laugh as she hit the floor and rolled to safety before coming to a crouch, watching him carefully. The son of a bitch wasn't even singed. He stood casually against the wall, once again protecting his back. She narrowed her eyes at the implied weakness.

She jumped to the side as another arc of disarming power flew toward her. Flames met it, outlining its strength and width as she rolled across the floor and sent a fireball as big as his head toward him at the same time.

He jumped out of the way, aiming again.

"You're getting old." She jumped the whip of power that would effectively still her own for up to hours at a time.

"Damned disarming shit. Figures you'd be a passive. Maybe *I'll* get to ride *you*." She threw a blade of static at his side, forcing him to glide further into the room as she rolled away from yet another disarming beam. "Dammit, don't you know how to do anything else? This is getting boring."

She jumped the next beam, timing the jump and her position. She threw a wall of flames, turned in mid-air and aimed a kick at his tall body. Her foot connected with his shoulder, throwing him off balance as she landed on her feet and attacked.

A quick kick to his stomach interrupted the next disarming force. A fist to his eye got the next one. She managed to land a strike to his kidneys, but even with the flames spreading around them, he caught on quickly.

She couldn't halt her cry when a blazing force of power collided with her head. Not his hand, but power. Pure, unadulterated psy-energy that threw her halfway across the room and left her shaking her head to clear her mind as she jumped to her feet.

Flames shot through the room, a shield around her, as several similar forms of flames flared in different areas. She kicked out as she passed him, only to have him catch her ankle and twist.

Recovering, Carmella flipped, intending to catch his jaw with the other foot but only glancing a blow off his shoulder as a dagger shaft of pain sliced through her arch.

"Bastard," she growled as the disarming force sizzled along her foot. Any higher and she would have been down.

He attacked then. His leg swept under her feet as they touched the floor, taking them out as she twisted at the last moment, catching her weight on her hands and flipping away from him. At the same time, she sent a charge of static electricity at what she hoped was his undefended back.

"Son of a bitch!" His curse had her smiling in triumph as she crouched, holding her weight on her knee, the other leg stretched out for balance and strength, her fingers touching the floor as she instantly assessed a point of attack.

She moved as he turned, giving her a chance at his broad back. Coming to her feet in a surge of power, she aimed for it as she anticipated the expected move for him to turn and protect it.

Sheer surprise shot through her as his arms suddenly surrounded her. Flames licked over her body, then extinguished as he chuckled.

A strangled scream escaped her throat as she felt him absorbing the power she was releasing, drawing it into his own body rather than being burned by the fiery waves.

She struggled against his hold, kicking back, slamming her head into his shoulder as he lifted her off her feet, his arms tightening around hers as he kept them clamped to her sides. Chuckling in victory, he lowered his head, his lips grazing her ear.

"Winner rules *and* rides," he growled. "My rules are I ride you."

# Chapter Nine

## ഇ

The naked lust in his voice seared her cunt. She couldn't escape his hold. No matter how she fought, wiggled or kicked back, he never faltered. She had never—not in her entire life—been so effectively overpowered. The feeling of helplessness, of utter submission, did nothing to stem the raging lust the fight had brought on. It made it worse.

"Bastard," she snarled, barely able to push the word past her lips as she fought for breath.

Flames built beneath her skin, but a second later sizzled out as the effects of a mental psychic blast suddenly paralyzed her. Her muscles went lax, despite the fury overwhelming her.

Damned psychic disarmer. She fought the numbing effects of the mental blast, determined she wouldn't give in. Not this easily. Damned cheat.

He grinned down at her as his hold shifted, one arm going behind her legs as he cradled her against his chest. She couldn't halt the shiver that raced through her body, had no way to tighten her muscles, steel her will against his effect on her. The force of the mental disarming relaxed every bone and muscle in her body while paralyzing the ability to move or to use the psychic abilities she possessed.

Disarmers were rare, but incredibly powerful.

"Now now, Carmella." He smiled down at her softly as he dropped her lightly on her bed and began undressing. "You made the rules, darling. I intend to fulfill them."

She could feel her breasts swelling as she struggled against the paralysis, willing strength back to her limbs so she could fight him, struggle, rip the clothes from his body. A fury of lust was rising inside her; where it came from she wasn't certain. But she wanted to test this man, tempt him, make him as wild for her as she was becoming for him.

"God, you're beautiful." His husky voice surprised her as he knelt, straddling her knees, his hard body rippling with muscle, the length and width of his cock causing her eyes to widen in surprise...in a tingle of feminine fear. "Tell you what. I'll make a deal with you. When I strip these pants off you, if you're not just as fucking wet as I am hard, then I'll let you be. Otherwise, you're mine, Carmella."

*Torren,* she whispered his name, torn between emotion and lust. She could feel him watching her, wanting her. He was aroused, his carnal excitement reaching out to her with surprising strength.

Her womb pulsed, her cunt igniting in a surge of need that left her breathless. She could feel her breasts throbbing as the nipples became tighter, harder, anticipating his touch to her body.

Her gaze flickered to the strength of his erection and she couldn't hold back a moan at the thought of him working it inside her, stretching her, possessing her. The thick root was as darkly fleshed as the rest of his body, as though he tanned in the nude. Heavily veined, the plum-shaped head throbbed erotically.

"Are you wet, Carma?" he asked softly as his hands went to the stretchy waistband of her form-fitting pants. "I bet you are. What do you think?"

She couldn't breathe, that was what she thought. His knuckles rasped against the flesh of her stomach as he began to ease the pants down her legs. She was defenseless. Unable to tighten against the excruciating pleasure of his touch, she could only lay there, feeling the shudders of pleasure work over her body as he undressed her.

*Torren!* The mental scream was desperate.

*It's okay, baby. He won't hurt you.* Despite the gentleness in his tone Carmella knew he was watching, feeling, knowing every word spoken, every touch.

She should be ashamed. Mortification should be searing her soul. Instead, her body responded with a blaze of heat that rocked her to her core.

Ryder's gaze became hooded, dark with hunger, as he stared down at her pussy. She thought he would speak, but he drew in a ragged breath instead as he moved to undress her. Her boots were unlaced and jerked from her feet along with the thick socks she wore beneath them. He pulled her pants quickly from her ankles, then moved to her upper body and worked the snug tank top over her head and arms, leaving her spread out before him.

"You're wet." He made it sound like an accusation, but his voice was hoarse with his own desire as he spread her thighs and moved between them once again.

Carmella was panting now. She could feel her juices flowing through her vagina, hot and slick, preparing her for him.

*Torren.* She felt lost, desperate. The pleasure searing over her body was terrifying her.

She felt him there, within her mind, sharing her pleasure in a way he never had before. The edge it gave to her own lust was razor sharp.

"I could take you now and you would love it." His hands smoothed up the outside of her thighs to her waist. "Are you tight, Carmella? Will I have to work my cock inside you or will it penetrate easily?"

She growled in desperation. She wished he would just do it. She didn't care how he achieved the penetration as long as he penetrated her.

"I bet you're as tight as a fist," he whispered as he leaned closer, his lips caressing hers. "I bet I have to work every inch inside you."

Oh yes. She shivered in anticipation as she watched him closely, slowly feeling the effects of the disarming beginning to ease. If he didn't hurry and start she was going to do it for him.

One hand moved caressingly along her side before cupping her breast slowly. His long fingers cupped the swollen mound before his thumb and forefinger moved to grip the nipple between them. Lightly. Oh God, she didn't want lightly. Carmella whimpered, the blood surging hard and fast through her veins as she fought to keep from begging.

"How do you like it, Carmella?" He licked her lips slowly, the heat of his tongue, the sensuous pleasure in the moist caress driving her insane. "Slow and easy, or hard and fast?" His fingers tightened on her nipple, pulling at it gently, working the flesh as sharp spears of pleasure drove into her womb.

She was within a second of having complete control of her body when he suddenly moved. She screamed out in anger as he flipped her to her stomach. Laughing—damn him—he was laughing as she began to struggle against him.

Carmella bucked, writhing beneath his harder, stronger body as she fought him. She was powerless. The touch of his skin, the very nature of his powers holding her own back, locking them inside her as they mixed with the surging lust screaming through her body.

"Say no, damn you." He nipped her ear as his legs tightened at her thighs, holding her still as she thrashed against him. "Say it, Carma. Now."

His cock nudged between her thighs, sliding in the thick cream her body had produced to ease his path.

She fought him as he tucked one hand beneath her, lifting her hips, holding them still as his cock kissed the entrance to her pussy.

"Do it," she nearly screamed. The heat of lust was driving her insane. Having him hold her despite her struggles, determined to take her, was nearly more than she could bear.

He chuckled, controlling her easily as she felt the head of his cock work into the entrance of her clenching cunt. Oh God. He was so big, so hot. She tightened as though to push him out, hearing his breath catch as her muscles clenched around the tip of the invader.

Her hand tightened in the blankets beneath her as she fought to find purchase against the mattress with her feet. She'd be damned if she would make it easy for him. She nearly bucked him from her for an agonizing second.

"Oh, that wasn't nice, Carma." His voice was strained. A second later he delivered a stinging smack to her rear.

Carmella stilled, whimpering at the dominant, forceful blow. Heat flared on the cheek of her ass, traveling directly to the building fire in her cunt. She stilled, panting, feeling the cream easing from her vagina as excitement blazed through her body. She had never known anything so damned hot. She had never felt so helpless and yet so feminine.

He wasn't trying to take anything she wasn't willing to give. Rather, he was taking her. Period.

His hand landed on her undefended ass again and she could only back into it, crying out as moisture covered her body and wave after wave of pleasure/pain streaked through.

He held her easily, the erotic spanking making her insane as she felt her flesh heat. From one rounded cheek to the other, his hand slapped with firm pressure that had her screaming in need.

"God, you look so pretty. Your sweet ass flushed and red." His voice was thick, filled with a dark male arousal that had her pussy creaming further.

"Do it," she cried out, shaking, needing the feel of his cock stretching her, invading her, more than she needed air to breathe.

"My rules," he whispered again, though his voice was strained, rough with his own lusts. He wasn't unaffected, his own control was stretching its limits, she thought deliriously. "God, you feel good, Carmella."

He held her hips as the head of his erection worked its way farther inside her heated pussy. She felt the muscles protesting, parting, little darts of sensual pain ravaging her system.

"Raise up." He pulled back on her hips with one hand as the other locked in her hair.

She wanted to scream out at the explicit dominance of the move as he moved her to the position he wanted her in. She was on her hands and knees, kneeling before him, her head arched back, her eyes widening in surprise at the erotic thrill of the forbidden.

She could feel Torren now. Ghostly fingers stroking her nipples as his excitement flared inside her. Oh God, it was too good.

*He's taking you, Carmella,* he whispered silently, erotically. *I can feel every sensation in your body. You love it. You love having him fucking you like this. Holding you down. Don't you?*

Carmella whimpered, dazed, confused by the overriding sensations building inside her as Torren made her more than aware of how much he liked the psychic voyeurism.

At the same time, Ryder pushed deeper into the quivering depths of her cunt, the width of his cock searing in the pleasure/pain of the penetration. She was so wet, so slick for him, she could hear the soft sounds of her flesh sucking him in, protesting any retreat.

"Ryder." Her back arched as the pressure on her hair intensified, drawing her back farther. "What the hell are you waiting for?"

"You." His voice was a hard growl as the short thrusts of his penis lodged him deeper inside her.

She was so full, stretched as tightly around him as a fist and glorying in each stroke of sensual heat it built in her body. She was shaking, whimpering, unable to protest anything he would want of her.

"Do you feel Torren, Carmella? Can you sense how much he likes feeling you get fucked? Getting taken?" Ryder's harsh words were followed by an abrupt powerful thrust of his hips that sent his cock burying into the very depths of her pussy.

"Yes," she screamed out in awareness, in ecstasy. It was too damned good. Too much.

She was impaled, empowered. She moaned weakly as she felt and heard both men cry out a second before Ryder lost control. His hand left her hair as both hands gripped her hips and his cock began to thrust hard and steady inside her gripping cunt.

She cried out, tortured, tormented by a pleasure that was more than she could have imagined.

She was helpless in the grip of Ryder's lust, her needs and Torren's pleasure. For the first time in Carmella's life a man had managed to best her. She felt small, helpless, feminine and in such heat she feared she would burn them all in the conflagration.

The muscles of her pussy clenched around Ryder's thrusting erection, aware of the fact that the act itself should have been humiliating, considering her lover was experiencing each sensation through his psychic connection to her.

"Yes," Ryder hissed behind her as she began to back into his thrusts, demanding more.

His hand smacked her rear again. Then again. Lost in the pleasure, in the forceful domination of the act, she could only cry out, pushing closer, demanding more.

"God, you're beautiful, Carmella." His voice was rough, almost broken. "And so fucking hot you're burning me alive."

And she didn't care. If the flames of who and what she was engulfed them all, she would have no regrets. At least, not if the building, pulsing knot of sensation in her womb was allowed freedom first.

Mindless, exacting, the pleasure built inside her with an intensity she could have never expected. Her clit was pulsing, swelling, even as her womb began to shudder with the shock of heated intensity flaring through her. She whimpered, losing herself and fighting to hold onto her sanity.

When the explosion came she knew in that one blinding instant she would never be the same. Her eyes widened as she heard Ryder encouraging her in the release. It erupted in her womb, then tightened and exploded in her pussy as she fought to hold back the flames building beneath her flesh.

Hard pulses of rapture shook her, threatening her mind and the last dregs of control as she flew apart beneath the rapid, forceful strokes inside her vagina.

She heard Ryder cry out, was aware of the hot, hot blasts of his semen deep inside her clutching cunt. She moaned instinctively though she knew she was dying, flying, coming apart in ways she could have never imagined as the pleasure disintegrated every cell in her body.

Carmella could only tremble in reaction as she felt Ryder ease her to the bed. Hard, warm arms wrapped around her, a broad chest cushioning her as her eyes closed in exhaustion so complete she didn't even think to fight it.

"Don't let me go." She shivered as she felt him pull the blanket over her.

"Never." She heard the whisper but wasn't certain if it was real or her imagination.

But his arms didn't let her go. His chest didn't move except for the soft rise and fall of his breathing. The hard body sheltering her didn't budge. She could sleep. For once in her life, Carmella felt safe.

\* \* \* \* \*

Ryder felt her slide into unconsciousness as she lay in his arms like warm, firm silk. Her hair flowed over his arm, her head rested against his chest. He breathed in deeply, tired, drained from the forceful release he had experienced inside her tight pussy.

Had he ever known pleasure that intense? Had another woman touched him so completely, so effectively, as this one did? He understood Torren's warnings then. The ones that cautioned him that dominating Carmella, mastering her and her powers, wouldn't be easy because her innocence, her needs, would sink into him so completely.

She had loved the thrill of the fight. Had relished being helpless in his arms, unable to escape. She had blazed as she felt Torren experiencing the act through their link. The added pleasure, the taste of the forbidden, had almost stolen her control. Almost, but not quite. He hadn't yet taken that last measure of strength she possessed.

I told you it wouldn't be easy. Torren's thought reflected his own regret. You'll have to be harder on her.

Ryder snorted. Why did I get the shit job, Torren? I have to piss her off so you can soothe her?

*It didn't bother him that this woman would belong, eventually, to both of them. What did bother him was that he would be the one to hurt her.*

She'll forgive you. She'll forgive us both in the end. It's the only way to prove you can master her, Ryder. She has to know it. She knows I can't do it alone. It wouldn't have done me any good to try. The job was always yours.

# Chapter Ten

## ℘

Carmella had never felt the "morning after" blitz of nerves and self-consciousness. She was usually out of bed long before any partner who dared to share it, and in control of herself. Show no weakness. She had been taught that rule early in life.

When she awoke hours later, wrapped in Ryder's arms, his heat and strength enveloping her, the subsequent emotions that followed held her still, silent, as she fought to make sense of them.

Ryder's legs were tangled with hers, one hard thigh pushed high between them. Her head was pillowed on his chest, one arm draped over his waist. It felt too right, too comfortable. And yet she felt hopelessly ensnared.

Torren was silent for now. She had gone to sleep with Ryder's arms wrapped around her and Torren's psychic energy soothing her. The unusual ménage had left her uncomfortable in the face of the once-again changing relationship with Torren. It left her feeling as though she were drowning when it came to Ryder, though.

Carmella wasn't a fool. She knew next to nothing about Ryder and she wasn't about to trust her life to this man just because the sex was great. And the sex *was* great. God, was it good. Thrilling, dominant, everything she had fantasized over for years. But that didn't mean she had to lose her head. And damn, Torren wasn't making this any easier on her.

"I can hear you thinking. You're going at it a mile a minute." Ryder's deep, warm voice stirred her senses. It was a caress, a stroke of longing over emotions she had fought for so many years.

The large, graceful hands that stroked over her back stirred more than just her senses. She could feel the arousal heightening. It was unfamiliar, confusing. She didn't like being affected so easily.

"Read thoughts too, do you?" Carmella moved to roll from his embrace, but his arms tightened around her as he pulled her beneath him, bracing himself on one arm as he rose to stare down at her.

"I can hear the static," Ryder whispered, his lips lowering to hers. "Let's see if I can give you something else to worry about."

His blue eyes glittered in stark, sensual arousal. Carmella felt her breath catch in her throat as the soft mat of his close-cropped beard caressed her cheek a second before he shifted yet again and his lips covered hers.

*It wasn't a hard, dominant kiss. Carmella trembled, her fingers clenched on his shoulders as his lips whispered over hers. Stroking, encouraging, asking permission in this, rather than taking.*

Confusion swamped her as she stared up at Ryder. He watched her curiously, his expression tender, a glimmer of humor, of heat in his eyes as his lips nudged against hers, parting them for the soft lick of his tongue.

Her heart was racing, emotions and confusion overwhelming her senses as he touched her so gently.

"You taste good, Carmella," he whispered against her lips, the caress firing nerve endings she didn't know she had.

His lips nudged against hers again, his beard rasping pleasantly against her skin, a warm roughened caress that had her shivering in response, fighting to breathe. Her gaze was locked by his, held mesmerized, ensnared by the brilliance of his desire, the warmth in his gaze.

Carmella could feel a whimper gathering in her throat and fought it back as his tongue licked against the seam of her lips once more. It was hot, heated silk and tempting desire. She couldn't deny the need to taste any longer.

Mouth watering, heart hammering, she touched her tongue to his. Her breath slammed in her chest as he stroked it, his gaze never leaving hers. Sensation speared through Carmella's body with the force of a tidal wave, leaving her shaking in the aftermath. Her womb clenched, her pussy ached. And still he stroked, nudged, teased her with those perfect, sensual lips.

Carmella fought the need to devour the taste of his mouth. The gentle, delicate stroking of her lips was too good to let go of. She had known only a few kisses, and never one like this. It was like ambrosia of the senses.

And Ryder wasn't unaffected either. His cheeks had turned a dull red, his eyes darkening, his breathing rough and heavy as his hands flexed, one in her hair, the other against her waist.

"Damn, you're sweet." Ryder broke the kiss, resting his forehead against hers as his chest rose and fell, hard and fast. "I could eat your lips like candy, Carmella."

"More." She couldn't resist the temptation.

She reached up, tangling her hands in the long strands of his thick hair as she tilted her head.

"More?" He licked at her lips as she nudged against his — close, but not what she needed.

"Ryder. Please." She arched closer as his palm stroked from her waist to her thigh and back again, and yet he still wasn't kissing her, wasn't satisfying the building need she had for his slow hunger.

"Please what?" he whispered against her lips, staring into her eyes as she fought to keep them open.

She tried to get closer to the teasing temptation of the kiss, but he only moved back, always just a breath from the touch she needed.

"Tell me what you want, Carmella."

What did she want? She didn't know. She wanted the sweet languor that had drifted through her senses at the tenderness he had given her moments ago.

"The kiss," she answered, hungry for more. "Please kiss me like that again. Soft. Like you mean it."

Ryder paused, a glimmer of surprise in his eyes a second before heat replaced it. His head lowered, his lips nuzzling against hers, and Carmella flinched from the pleasure.

She couldn't hold back the whimper now. She couldn't still the overpowering, unfamiliar need rising in her chest like a greedy beast gasping in desperation for more.

The sweet ache traveled to her swollen breasts, her hard, inflamed nipples. It washed beneath her flesh, across her abdomen, then down to strike ruthlessly at her tender clit, her weeping pussy. Carmella twisted against him, reveling in the soft stroke of his lips and tongue as her eyes closed, too heavy, too caught in the web of arousal he was spinning around her.

"Yes, baby," he soothed, his voice hoarse, his own control sounding strained. "Feel how good it is, Carmella. How good it can be. You're burning me alive."

Carmella could feel the tautness of his body against her, the fine film of perspiration that gathered along his flesh. The knowledge that it was affecting him as greatly as it was her made the intensity deepen, strengthen.

Emotion swelled inside her. Blistering, frightening, as he cradled her body closer to his own, the light mat of dark blond hair on his chest rasping her tender breasts.

"I need more, baby," he growled, his breath panting from his chest. "Let me have you. Let me in, darlin'."

She lifted her eyelids, staring up at him as he watched her with drowsy sensuality. He was asking her? Had anyone ever asked her?

Carmella couldn't hold back her cry as her lips parted for him. What came next shocked her senses, tightened every cell in her body. His tongue pressed into her slowly, stroking over

74

hers as his head tilted, his lips covering hers with tortured restraint.

Heat enveloped her; so sensual, so evocative, she could only tremble against the sensations moving through her. Ryder seemed no less helpless in the grip of the flood of pleasure. His body was tense, tight, as he fought the carnal demands to experience the almost innocent sweetness of the caress.

The hunger raged just beneath the surface, though. The inferno of demand was only stoked higher, hotter as they fought their bodies' demands to ease the building arousal in exchange for the agonizingly gentle caress of lips upon lips, tongues stroking, learning, tasting.

# Chapter Eleven

ဢ

The silky warmth of Ryder's beard caressed her cheek as his head tilted again, deepening the kiss further. Carmella's nipples were roughened by his chest hair, sending flares of sensation rioting through her body. It was the most erotic, most sensual act she had ever known in her life.

"Ambrosia," he whispered as his lips slid from hers, his beard rasping her skin as his lips trailed across her cheek, along her neck.

His hand wasn't still either. It cupped her breast, his thumb and forefinger catching a nipple firmly between them as Carmella arched into the touch. She couldn't process the complete sensory overload that gripped her body. Pleasure, hot and sweet, twisted through her womb, making her pussy weep in need.

"Ryder." She sighed his name. Needed to hear it, needed to know it was real. She fought to hold back her agonized pleas as the sensual ache built between her thighs.

"Carmella," he answered her, his tone wicked as his head lowered to lick a thrusting nipple.

Carmella jerked against him, drawing in a shattered breath as the pleasure curled around the tip before streaking to her sensitive womb and causing it to spasm with the strength of the sensation.

Before she could recover he enveloped the hard peak in the heated cavern of his mouth before his lips closed around it, drawing on it with a lazy hunger that had her hands clenching tightly in the hair close to his scalp as she fought to hold onto sanity.

She trembled, shuddered from the force of the pleasure, as she fought to sort through the emotions tormenting her now.

"This is killing me." She twisted against him as he suckled at her breast, his tongue laving it, curling around it as though her nipple was a favorite sweet treat.

"Will you die happy then?" he asked her lazily as he began to kiss a path down her perspiration-slick stomach toward the moist ache between her thighs. The heated throb there was a physical pain. The muscles of her cunt clenched in hunger as the building sensation in her clit drove her higher toward the mindless pursuit of release.

"I'll die happy," she moaned weakly as he moved down her body, parting her thighs, his fingers sifting through the tiny, desire-soaked curls that covered the mound of her cunt. "Just let me come."

"Not yet." He licked into her belly button, murmuring his appreciation of her as his lips continued their path of discovery to her aching pussy. "I want to taste you this time, Carmella. All of you."

A second after he spoke his tongue swiped through the slit of her pussy with a caress so destructive she nearly exploded. His tongue rasped the swelling pearl of her clit, sending sparks of sensation tearing through her body.

"God, Ryder." Her hips arched, her hands moving from his hair to tangle in the blankets of the bed. God forbid that in her pleasure she should pull his head away from her with her desperate grip.

It was so damned good. His tongue worked its way slowly along the soaked slit, probing, teasing, drawing yet more of the frothing cream from her pussy. Her body was tight, her flesh tingling as he ate at the tender curves of her cunt, making her insane for more. Making her insane to come. She could feel the inferno building in her womb, through her pussy, her clit. She writhed beneath his careful strokes, fighting to draw him closer to the little bud tormenting her with its need.

"Stop teasing me," she panted as he skirted around her clit once again and moved lower to lick at the juices spilling from her vagina. "I can't stand it, Ryder."

"You're so good, Carmella. So sweet and hot." He was breathing hard, fast, his voice rough with his own arousal. "I could eat this sweet pussy all day long."

She cried out as his tongue dipped into the well of her cunt, thrusting deep and hard inside her, the gentle rasp of his beard adding to the erotic sensations with an intensity that left her breathless.

He caressed her pussy as he had her lips. Smoothing over the inner folds, his tongue licking, flicking at the hungry mouth of her vagina as he tormented her into mindless lust.

Then he licked up again, circling her clit, coming closer to the swollen bead but never really giving her the relief she needed. Then his mouth covered it as he suckled it between his lips, his tongue rasping, hot, fiery strokes that destroyed her.

Her orgasm tore through her with the strength of a hurricane. Velvet waves of sensation flooded her entire being, tightening her body further, forcing a shocked scream past her lips.

Before she could recover, before the last violent vibration of release could ease, Ryder was rising between her thighs, coming over her, his lips covering hers as his cock began to ease into the tight tunnel of her cunt.

She tasted her juices on his lips. It was tangy, with just a hint of an earthy musk as his tongue speared deep into her mouth, his erection working inside her pussy.

He filled her slowly, pausing as he settled into the cradle of her thighs, the head of his cock pressing deep and hard into the very depths of her cunt. Carmella shuddered at the pleasure, the need rising inside her once again. His gentle lovemaking was more than she could bear. Never had she known such depths of arousal, such deep, all-consuming pleasure as what she felt now.

"I can't wait," he whispered, his voice rough, his lips moving over hers with an edge of desperation. "Now, Carma, I can't wait any longer."

And he took her. Carmella cried out as his cock retreated then pushed back in a hard, soul-destroying stroke. His hands gripped her thighs, raising them, pushing her legs back to open her further for his invasion as he began to fuck her with an almost mindless rhythm.

He stretched her, filled her. Each stroke was a lash of shattering pleasure inside her pussy, deep in her womb until she was begging, pleading, needing him harder, faster, needing the release building inside her with a desperation that terrified her.

Ryder was groaning into her neck now, biting her sensually, before licking over the small mark, kissing it, driving her insane with the added touch. His body flexed, bowed, his muscles rippling beneath her hands as she gripped his shoulders, holding on as he rode her through the driving need for release.

When it came, Carmella swore she was dying. Her eyes flew open, widened, her breath halting in her throat a second before a low, tremulous wail issued from her.

"Yes, Carma," he groaned. "Come around me, baby. Come for me, Carma..."

His harsh male cry joined her in the symphony of rapture. Carmella felt him tighten, his cock jerking, his hot seed spilling inside the depths of her vagina in heated spurts. And still he thrust, stroked, driving her through her orgasm as she cried out his name.

The aftermath came slowly. Shocks of pleasure echoed through Carmella's body as Ryder collapsed beside her, drawing her against his moist chest as he too fought for breath, for recovery. It was a unique feeling for her. A sense of security, of warmth, and one she wanted to hold onto for a long time to come.

*And Carmella fought for understanding. Because she knew, deep in her soul, that when she lost Ryder – and she would lose him – it would destroy a part of her. He completed her. Fulfilled her. How would she ever be able to accept less again?*

# Chapter Twelve

ॐ

*I was less then?* Torren. Amusement crackled in the intrusive thought as Carmella heard his voice echo through her head, answering to her last thought. He had been amazingly silent as Ryder had taken her, yet she was aware now that he had been experiencing each second of it.

*I'll find you soon.* She didn't tell Ryder she had made contact. For a moment she wondered if he knew how close Torren was to her thoughts at all times.

Follow Ryder. The command was harsh, uncompromising. He'll find me. You have to do this his way, Carmella.

Dammit, Torren. What are you getting me into? She cursed silently. He knew you were there last night. He knows you shared it.

Of course he does. She felt his soft sigh. There are things you don't know, Carmella. Just be careful. Do as Ryder tells you.

She snorted silently. She didn't think so.

"I have to shower." Carmella tried to pull herself from Ryder's arms. She needed to escape his touch so she could make sense of her own confusion, her own fears.

Something wasn't right here. Something wasn't making sense and she hated her own suspicions worse than anything, because she had a very bad feeling Torren knew a hell of a lot more than he was saying.

"Do you think I don't know he contacted you just now, Carmella?" Ryder asked her softly, his voice almost menacing.

"I can feel his energy all around you. You don't have to hide it."

Confusion filled her as he watched her. His gaze speared into her, accusing and harsh.

"I don't know you. If you're who you're supposed to be, then we'll reach Torren with no problems," she whispered. "I can't just trust…"

"Don't know me?" he snarled. "If you don't know me, damn you, it's because you refuse to look."

He pushed himself from the bed, turning his back on her; displaying the most delectable male ass she had ever laid eyes on. Smooth, firm, curved so temptingly it made her hands itch to cup it. Damn. How had she missed seeing his backside? It was a fucking work of art.

"Stop staring at my ass like that." His voice was a rough, angry growl.

"Why?" She laid back on the bed, a flare of regret rushing through her as he dragged his pants up his well-muscled legs. "It's damned fine looking."

"Get a shower." He didn't comment on her appreciation of his male form. "I'll go back to my room and shower. I'll meet you back here so we can head for Torren's location."

She frowned at that, raising up on her elbows as she watched him.

"Then you do know where he is?" Which meant Torren knew the location as well. "He's not with PSI, is he?"

He paused, the muscles of his back tightening at the question as he turned from her.

"PSI hasn't taken him. Yet."

Silence stretched between them for long, tense moments. Carmella rose slowly from the bed, watching Ryder carefully.

"Where is he and how long has he been there?"

"He's several days from here, but getting there won't be easy, Carmella. You have to trust me. Implicitly."

Carmella picked up the towel she had thrown across a chair the night before and wrapped it slowly around her naked, sensitive body.

"Trust you, huh?" she asked him softly as he turned to meet her gaze. "And how am I supposed to do that? You've given me very little reason to do so."

His expression was somber, quiet. "I've given you more than I've ever given anyone else, Carmella."

She drew in a deep, hard breath. There was something about the way he said it, the regretful tone of his voice, a glimmer of longing in his eyes that threw her off balance, made her want to trust him. Made her want to give him everything, anything he needed.

She looked away from him, fighting her needs, what she saw as his needs.

"I'm sorry," she whispered finally, shaking her head. "Trust isn't just given..."

"Spare me, Carmella." He jerked his shirt on, then his boots, lacing them quickly. "We can't wait around here any longer. We leave tonight. Get ready to go."

"Ryder." She stopped him as he reached the door.

He paused, turning to her slowly. His expression was hard, fierce, his eyes glittering with suppressed anger.

"Did you know where Torren was all along?" she asked him, hating the suspicion forming in her mind.

His lips twisted in amused mockery. "I know many things, Carmella. If you would take the time to learn how to look, so would you."

He stalked from the room and, seconds later, she heard the door slam with an abrupt, sharp sound. She winced, getting the feeling he was a bit too restrained in the way he closed the door.

\* \* \* \* \*

Ryder stalked down the short distance between his room and Carmella's, slamming his own door viciously behind him. Son of a bitch, this was more complicated than he had wanted it to be. He hadn't wanted to get this close to her this fast. Hell, he hadn't wanted to get this close to her period.

He shook his head at his own ignorance.

I told you she wasn't the trusting type. Torren growled the dark thought. Dammit, of course she's suspicious.

She had the chance to bond with me, Torren, he snarled silently. While I took her, she could have opened up.

It grated that she hadn't. That she had fought the final acceptance of her heart. Without it, he would never regain her trust once she learned his deception. And yet he knew that the moment she opened herself to him, she would know the lies. It was a double-edged sword and one that left him a little pissed off.

She had the same chance with me many times, Ryder. It will come when it's meant to.

Ryder could sense Torren's frustration, his impatience. The end of this debacle was nearing and he knew they both looked forward to its conclusion.

Dammit, I never thought I'd end up sharing the woman I loved, and not regretting it, Ryder finally groused silently. Damned good thing it's you, Torren. I'd have to kill anyone else.

Yeah. Same goes. Torren's mocking laughter had Ryder's lips kicking up in a grin.

They were both possessive bastards. They always had been. It amazed him that the thought of sharing Carmella didn't fill him with fury. But, he had known Torren was a part of her from the first touch he had made to her mind. She loved him, yet the love was incomplete. That had changed when she awoke in Ryder's arms. As though her heart, her woman's soul, had been waiting for the last piece of the puzzle to be complete. It was strange as hell.

84

Hurry and get her here. Torren was running out of patience. Our time's running out and Reidel has already contacted me twice for an update. The third time she'll start making demands.

Reidel was likely already doing so.

We'll leave within an hour or so, Ryder promised as he headed to the shower. I want to get this completed as quickly as possible. Carmella's frustration only fed his, made his sexual hunger for her darker, more intense.

I'll be waiting for you. Torren's impatience was beginning to affect him now. Between him and Carmella, Ryder's own emotions surged hotter, more volatile than before.

Ryder felt the psychic tie disconnect and he sighed wearily as he stepped in the shower and turned the lukewarm water on full blast. Son of a bitch, if life wasn't getting too damned complicated.

# Chapter Thirteen

ဢ

"Where are we headed?" Carmella closed the door to the fairly new land and water Hummer.

The new motors, created just before the fall of the psychic government fifty years before, were powered by energy-rich sun crystals. Discovered deep within the earth's surface, the crystals, once exposed to the sun for several years, trapped a reusable solar power within the many faceted chambers they held.

The cloudy gray crystals, once energized, were nearly as clear and perfect as diamonds. The discovery had rocked the energy-poor world at the time. Fossil fuels were nearly exhausted, and only the most powerful of the citizens could afford the minute amount of electricity being generated.

"We're headed south," Ryder told her quietly as he engaged the motor and pulled away from the inn. "We'll cross the river outside town and head into West Virginia. I want to stick fairly close to the coast, though it will make the trip longer than it would be going straight through."

"And we'll end up where?" she asked him patiently.

His hands tightened on the steering wheel as he glanced at her.

"Figure it out," he finally suggested with a shrug of his shoulders.

Carmella sighed heavily as she sat back in her seat. Men amazed her. He acted like a betrayed lover. What the hell did he want? She thought only women pouted when the commitment thing became an issue. And it wasn't like she actually balked at. She just wasn't willing to trusting the man without proof. Good sex did not always mean a good relationship. But, damn, if it wasn't really good sex.

"Reading minds isn't one of my talents, Ryder." Though she admitted it would sure as hell come in handy right now.

"Reading me could be," he told her, his voice clipped, cool. "If you wanted to."

She glanced at him a bit mockingly. "I can imagine the perverted things that run through your head," she grunted. "I don't need to be a mind reader for that one."

She watched his lips thin and shook her head in irritation. He was worse than a damned female virgin looking for commitment. What the hell was wrong with him? She didn't need another man complicating her life, making her question herself on a daily basis. Torren did just fine with that, and she didn't have to tolerate him as a lover anymore to boot.

Not that she had to tolerate Ryder exactly. Her cunt ached at the thought of his penetration, his thick, heavily veined cock working inside her, stretching her, filling her.

She barely controlled the shiver of arousal that would have shuddered over her body.

"Get ready." Ryder's voice was cool as he headed the Hummer out of town. "We'll be crossing the river at the old shipping docks just after dark. It could get hairy."

As he spoke, he touched one of the controls on the dash, activating the virtual screen on the windshield that was used in place of headlights. Instantly, a colorized, crisp view was reflected back at them. The windows at the side of the door darkened further, enclosing them within a cocoon of intimacy that had Carmella instantly wary.

She had been similarly enclosed in vehicles before. With Torren, and on occasion, other men they worked with. She never felt the hot, anticipatory surge of arousal that flushed her body now, though.

Carmella stared at the view screen in front of them, showing the silent streets. There were few lights as the land slowly darkened, but the heat and motion detector on the screen easily picked out the bodies lurking in what would have otherwise been shadows.

The night folk were getting ready to move in—the vigilantes, the psychic rebels, the predators of the fallen city. What had once been a thriving, profitable area had been turned into a rubble-filled hellhole.

The rebuilding had begun in what was considered the upper portion. There, the more affluent citizens had managed to keep themselves protected with guards, heavy iron fences and attack dogs. Now, the upper district was watched with jealousy and fury. Once again the less privileged were losing out to those who were protecting themselves with the added help.

The best food went to their markets. Markets that the lesser citizens were not allowed entrance to. The scraps, the decayed portions left days later, were then shipped to the downtown district. It was this lack of equality that had first given the psychic government a hold on the land. A promise to keep the land equal. To use their gifts to stop corruption and crime. It had bred the worst wars the world had ever known.

"Why aren't you using the old bridge?" she asked as the Hummer turned along one of the broken streets and bumped its way toward the old docks.

Ryder glanced over at her as he maneuvered between the collapsing buildings and deeply pitted path that had once been a wide, well-paved road.

"A heavily armed, well-equipped Hummer traveling over that bridge would be hard to miss," he told her quietly. "The bridges are watched by both PSI agents and vigilante forces, especially at night. I want to avoid as many as possible."

"There's no way to hide a damned tank, Ryder," she said. "And you're heading into one of the worst areas imaginable. West Virginia won't be easy to get through undetected."

"We'll be well protected." He didn't sound unduly concerned. "After we pass through West Virginia the going will be easier. Many of the lower states are building back faster than they are in the north. Same can be said for parts of the west. Evidently, the pioneer spirit is still alive and well."

That didn't surprise Carmella in the least. She remembered her grandmother's tales of the areas he was talking about. Strong, determined men and women would rebuild. She'd heard that in the south the psychic witch-hunts had ended decades before because most of the citizens had natural talent. Enough that they didn't outright kill unless it was needed.

"Many of Tyre's followers were said to have headed for the Keys," she said then, whispering the dreaded name as she fought the fear in her chest. "They never found Tyre's body, did they? Or the Tyrea's?"

"No. They thought the Tyrea still lived after the government fell. But no one was certain."

The Tyrea was said to have possessed the powers of all the elements. Fire, wind and rain. She had been the most feared of the psychics, and rumor was that she had also been the one who finally turned the tide in the last bitter wars.

"Do you think he's still alive?" It was her greatest fear, that he lived.

"No, I don't think he is," Ryder finally breathed out. "He was just a man, Carmella. An extra-ordinary man. A man driven insane by the manipulations to his brain. Like the rest of them, he couldn't control the fallout."

"And what of those who are his descendants?" she asked him, praying her voice was even, that the fears that filled her were hidden.

"I don't know." He glanced at her, his look intent. "There were over two hundred of the bastards to begin with. Before they were taken out, there were ten times that many. Who knows what happened or the repercussions that came of it?

According to tests later, the children of the original group had no insanity, merely a lust for power. Those who didn't became rebels were marked for death by their brothers and their fathers."

The last decade of the wars had been horrendous.

"Those of Tyre's line are automatically killed, even now," she pointed out.

He sighed wearily. "That wouldn't benefit the new government in any way," he said softly. "Too many of us, especially the stronger psychics, can make that link. We can only pray that one day the horror will ease, and somehow, we'll find a middle ground again."

Carmella stared at the view screen, knowing full night would have fallen, the darkness obscuring the desperation of a land torn apart. Her grandmother had warned her, in those days before she split her apart from the two sisters Carmella had idolized. They were each of the Tyre. To survive, they would have to be separated.

She hadn't seen her sisters since she was ten. She had lost her grandmother, and she couldn't even remember her parents.

"We're moving into the dock area," Ryder warned her. "After we cross the river it should be pretty smooth."

The river was a mess. It moved with a strong current, though it was said to be much lower now than it had been more than a hundred years previously. Below the surface the possibility of disaster waited. Washouts from farther upriver had collected all manner of debris. Broken bridges, the hulking remains of sunken ships and a shattered society lay in wait.

They moved into the water slowly as Ryder activated the marine propeller at the back of the vehicle, and the airtight locks on the motor and doors. Artificial air began to instantly pump into the small confines as the Hummer became a mini motorboat moving into the murky depths of the less than secure Ohio River.

# Chapter Fourteen

**ဢ**

"Are you ever going to stop pouting?" Carmella asked him hours later as the vehicle sped across the deserted, fairly intact highway Ryder had chosen as their route to wherever the hell they were going.

She turned in her seat watching his brooding expression. It was really rather cute, she thought. He was trying not to actually pout, but his expression was one of pure male offended ego. The lowered brows, the narrowed set of his eyelids, the firm line of his mouth. He wasn't pleased with her. He had been upset ever since the confrontation at her room in the inn.

"I do not pout, Carmella." He flicked a glance at her out of the corner of his eyes as he navigated the vehicle using the virtual screen in front of him. "I'm concentrating."

She looked at the dash. The impressive display showed radar tracking, speed, and a small directional map with part of the course laid out.

"Concentrating on what?" She unclipped the belt that strapped across her shoulders and waist so she could lean more comfortably against the door and watch him. "Looks like the vehicle does most of the work."

Ryder grunted. "They cost enough. They should."

Carmella frowned at a sudden thought. "How did you manage to get a state of the art Hummer and still keep the skin on your back?" she asked him suspiciously. "Takes a lot of cash to acquire one of these babies."

"I had the funds. I wanted it." He shrugged easily.

"Why would you want it?" She didn't like the suspicions rising in her mind. "Why would you need it? Why not a smaller one?"

"You're a very suspicious woman, Carmella." A small smile tilted his lips. She felt her womb clench in response to the look of complete male confidence. It was too sexy by far.

"I'm still alive because of it." She was betting he could write the book on how to be an aggravating psychic male.

"Possibly." His smile flashed in the dim light of the vehicle. "If you want answers you're going to have to do better than that, though."

"You know, Ryder, you betray me and I won't be a happy person." She felt the need to warn him of this. "The last son of a bitch who tried to sell me out to a PSI agent is rotting somewhere in hell. I don't think you want to join him."

Actually, he was most likely nursing more than one burn scar, but she felt a tough attitude starting out might be important with Ryder.

He smiled again as he glanced at her. The rakish, devil-may-care grin immediately set her hackles up.

"I'm a disarmer, baby, and an absorber," he reminded her. "And a damned good one. Better make sure you do it right the first time you try, because if you don't, it's your ass that will pay the price."

She frowned with what she hoped was fierce severity. "What does that mean?"

"It means I'll set your ass on fire if you even attempt anything so asinine towards me again. A little harmless tussle is one thing. You try to blindside me and I'll take it seriously."

"Excuse me?" She blinked incredulously. "A harmless tussle? Is that what you call it? If you hadn't cheated with that shield someone was helping you keep around you I would have fried your ass."

"Uh huh," he agreed lazily as he flipped one of the many buttons on the middle of the steering wheel before taking his hands off it to stretch in indulgent unconcern. "You convince yourself of that, darlin', if you have to. But I know better."

"What do you mean by that?" She crossed her arms beneath her breasts, ignoring the heavy lidded look he gave the full mounds, as well as the way her nipples hardened and peaked for his appraisal.

"It means we both know better," he growled. "Take your shirt off."

She blinked at him in surprise. She felt her body tense, tighten, at the darker tone of his voice, the sexual intensity that filled it. She glanced at the display on the virtual screen. The vehicle was evidently on some sort of autopilot, because his hands were busy loosening his pants rather than steering.

Carmella was aware of the fact that somewhere along the line the subject had been diverted, but with the heat building in her cunt and the arousal clawing at her womb, she decided to tackle it later. Now, alone in the vehicle, darkness surrounded them and the time to enjoy the hard body in the seat across from her was too much to resist. She pulled her shirt off as he directed.

"God love us," he seemed to pray as her breasts were bared before his eyes. "You make me lose my mind, Carmella."

He pushed his seat farther back, reclining it fully, creating a bed of sorts. Searching the side of her seat for the lever, Carmella did the same.

Ryder raised a narrow padded extension from the floor that fitted between the two wide bucket seats, making a complete bed. Carmella raised her brows in surprise. "Nice," she murmured.

"Effective," he corrected. "Undress."

"Demanding, aren't you?" she suggested, fighting to keep the smile from her voice.

The dominance in his tone did something to her that she knew it shouldn't. It turned her on, made her weak with arousal, with need. She had never known such a level of excitement before Ryder. She feared she never would again with any other man. There was something different about Ryder. Something that reached deeper than the physical, and that terrified her more than the thought of betrayal did.

"I can be more than demanding, Carma." His voice whispered over her senses as he pulled his boots and pants off before coming to his knees.

Carmella had just pulled her own off, and turned back to him, when his hands caught in her hair and he lowered his head to take her lips in a rapacious kiss. She moaned into the blistering, demanding possession. Her mouth opened for his spearing tongue as she met it with her own. They clashed in a duel of lust and need that had her quivering in anticipation.

Ryder didn't ask for anything. He was surging with lust, his body tense with it, hungry for her response. That knowledge had her heart swelling with feelings she didn't want to recognize. And somewhere deeper, she felt a connection, a bond to him that burned hotter than mere emotion.

His kiss was like a flame itself. Hot and moist, his lips and tongue stroking, tasting, drawing her deeper into the inferno *he* was creating, rather than her. Her hands moved to his neck, releasing the small leather thong that held the thick strands back from his face. As it fell forward, she moaned in satisfaction, in pleasure. Until he drew back from her.

She bit at his lips as he pulled away, needing more. His kiss was like an elixir of passion. She was becoming addicted. But what he presented seconds later wasn't bad either.

He rose before her, his knees on the makeshift bed, his head bending low to accommodate the roof of the Hummer as his cock nudged at her lips. His moan was a rough, demanding growl as her lips opened, her mouth covering the bulging head as her tongue stroked the underside hungrily.

94

"Yes, baby," he whispered roughly, his fingers tunneling into her hair, clenching on the strands to hold her in place. "Your mouth is damned near as hot as your sweet cunt."

She tightened on him, suckling slowly at the turgid flesh, feeling the hard throb of lust that pulsed just under the velvety skin. She stroked the satin expanse of extra-sensitive skin just under the head of his erection, glorying in his strangled moan as she did so.

She wrapped her fingers around the thick shaft, caressing the bold shape of his cock as she sucked as much as possible into her mouth. He tasted of heat and desire, of hard hot male and aching passion and Carmella couldn't get enough of him.

She drew slowly, wickedly, on the throbbing cock, feeling the slick dampness of his pre-cum as he moaned in pleasure above her.

"Yeah," he sighed roughly as she tongued the head. "So good, Carmella. Your mouth is so damned good."

His fingers clenched tighter in her hair, his breath rasping in his throat as she licked and suckled his cock like a favorite treat. And it was. A treat she had never known. Clean, male passion—hot and rich—making her body tighten, making her heart swell with each rough groan from his chest.

He held himself still as her lips moved over him, stroking him. Her tongue whipped across the sensitive underside, probing beneath the flared head before suckling him in hard and deep once again.

"I want to come in your sweet mouth, Carmella," he groaned out explicitly, his cock throbbing in warning of the eminent release. "I want to feel you sucking the life out of me."

Carmella whimpered. She suckled harder, faster, feeling him begin to move, to fuck her mouth with quick, hard thrusts as his body tightened. His hands held her head still, steady. She could feel his gaze on her, the naked lust she knew would fill it urging her on.

Her hands stroked the now damp shaft, her lips tightening as his thrusts became harder, faster. She was starved for him. The taste of him, the heat of his ejaculation.

When it came, she moaned as deeply as he did. Hard, fierce jets of rich semen spurted into her throat as he drove his cock as deep between her lips as he dared. He trembled, biting off a rough curse, holding her head firmly in place as he shot another thick stream of his seed inside her mouth.

His muscles were bunched, his cock twitching and throbbing in her hands as he moaned her name. Carmella cried out, the sound throttled, hoarse with need as she licked the flared head clean of the last trace of his semen.

"God, you're going to kill me." He was still hard, his cock still pulsing with life as he drew back from her. "You make me crazy, Carmella."

# Chapter Fifteen

ॐ

Carmella lay back on the surprisingly comfortable bed the seats had made, staring up at Ryder as he moved between her thighs. Her body was sensitized, primed for his possession. The empty ache in her pussy was mind destroying, desperate. She needed him now. No preliminaries, no hesitations.

Her hips arched for just that, a cry tearing from her throat as she felt the head of his cock at the weeping entrance of her cunt. He pushed into her slowly, stretching the sensitive tissue with exquisite pleasure-pain as he worked his cock into her.

Carmella arched into him, fighting for breath as the erotic intensity rippled through her body. She was on fire for him. Her flesh heated as her need became desperate, so close to orgasm she could feel her womb tightening in preparation for it.

She stared up at Ryder, the brooding sexuality in his features shadowed by the dim lights of the virtual windshield, his blue eyes glittering with passion, his bearded face appearing rough, rakish, as he watched her vagina swallow the thick length of his cock.

It was amazing, shattering, the sensations that rocked over her body as he thrust inside her. The piercing pleasure of the slow thrusts had her panting for more as his erection widened the small entrance. Each inch was an agonizing pleasure as she waited for the moment he would fill her completely.

Her pussy ached, throbbed. The tissue, sensitive to every touch, echoed with the hard pulse of his cock as he filled her, heating her vagina, increasing the sensitivity of the inner channel.

"I could fuck you forever." His voice was a harsh, dark growl. "You're so hot and tight around my cock it's all I can do not to come inside you now."

"Did I ask you to wait?" She could barely speak for the rioting waves of pleasure washing through her body. "Oh God, Ryder, don't wait."

He slid into her to the hilt. She could feel the head of his cock throbbing, flexing in the depths of her pussy, making her insane to feel him moving, thrusting hard and deep inside her.

He bent over, one arm bracing her shoulder, the other wrapping beneath her as he covered her. His weight was a sensually heated blanket of desire. Every touch of his body along hers stroked nerve endings, awakening them to the pleasure of his touch.

Carmella could feel the blood singing through her veins, throbbing in an explicit demand for his driving thrusts. Her hands rose to his shoulders, clenching the hard muscles that tightened beneath her touch. Her head lowered, her lips caressing his chest, her tongue stroking, licking at his skin as he groaned above her.

"Leave me some control." He was panting as his hips flexed, pressing his cock deeper into the sensitive tissue that cupped his flesh.

She bit at his chest. Her teeth nipped, her tongue stroked as he moaned in defeat. He began to move in long, slow thrusts that had her crying out in clawing hunger. She had never known passion so intense, lust so hot and all consuming.

"Do it," she cried out breathlessly, her hips writhing beneath him as he stroked slowly into her body. "Please, Ryder, fuck me."

One broad hand tunneled into her hair, the other gripping her hips tightly to hold her in place as he drove her insane with the deep, slow strokes into her pussy. She could feel her moisture there gathering, frothing, creaming with the blistering carnal hunger flaying her body.

"God, you're so soft and tight," he whispered at her ear, his breathing hard and quick. "I don't want to come, Carmella. I don't want to ever stop fucking you."

She lifted her legs, clamping them around his waist as he rode her with a leisurely pace. It wasn't enough. It was driving her crazy, making her scream, her voice hoarse with the arousal pounding through her veins.

Their flesh was slick with the effects of the lust burning through their systems, the smell of sex, the sound of suckling female tissue and hard driving male filling the interior of the vehicle.

"If you don't move your ass, I'm going to burn blisters on it." She tried to scream her outrage that he was deliberately, cruelly taunting her, but the words only came out as a gasping plea.

She tightened the muscles of her cunt around his invading erection, feeling her flesh ripple around him as he groaned hard and deep in her ear. It was effective. He began to move harder, faster, holding her still beneath him as the pleasure intensified to a level bordering pain.

Carmella gasped for breath, feeling the surging sensations gathering in her womb, tightening it as her pussy clenched around Ryder's thrusting cock. Slowly, every cell in her body became taut, sensitized, hot...

Her eyes flew open as the surging orgasm exploded low in her stomach and began to rush through her body. Her wailing cry was forced from her throat, the hard pulse of her release gushing through her cunt. Ryder moaned thickly, his body stiffening, his own climax tearing through his body.

It felt never-ending. Rippling and surging, a tidal wave of intensity that swept past her control, her shields and her blocks, leaving her open. Aware. Broken.

He had betrayed her. In that one blinding moment when the heart and soul opened, connecting with Ryder's, Carmella knew a sweeping, all consuming rush of fury and pain. The son of a bitch had betrayed her.

The orgasm rushing through her had barely stilled before fire erupted from her hands, sweeping down his back only to be absorbed just as quickly by his body.

Hard hands slammed her wrists to the makeshift bed as she screamed out her fury, twisting beneath him, desperate to be released.

"You bastards!" She cursed him and Torren together. "You son of a bitch bastards, I'll kill you."

Carmella stared up at Ryder's hard, savage features as he held her down easily. His eyes were narrowed, his expression calm, stern. His cock was still lodged inside her, hot and thick, despite his release.

"You have lousy timing," he told her softly as she felt bands of power encircling her body, holding her still, defenseless, as he moved back from her body.

"Fucking PSI agent." She shook her head as bitterness overwhelmed her. "You and Torren both. You betrayed me, Ryder."

She struggled against the bonds, hating herself for trusting him or Torren, but hating them more. She fought her tears. Damn them, she would not cry over either of them.

"Amazing how you can see only those things you want to see," he remarked as he got dressed.

The Hummer moved along the road, growing steadily closer to their destination, to Torren. She knew now why her commander had been so damned hard to find, why he had sent Ryder to her. The elaborate plot made her almost as sick as the truth she had glimpsed in Ryder's soul.

The unique shield that all Fyrebrands possessed had only one key. There was one way to see into her soul, into the part of her that could never lie, even to herself. That key was love. Only a true disarmer would reach the lock and use that emotion to open the doors into her heart. But in doing so, she had glimpsed his as well. What she saw destroyed her.

He hadn't just betrayed her. She ignored the love staring her in the face, the need and the dreams. She had seen the betrayal, the truth of why he had come for her. As judge and jury. As the last step between her and death. She had seen that her secret was no longer safe, even from herself. And she knew, in one blinding second, that none of it mattered without trust. And Ryder didn't trust her.

# Chapter Sixteen

ဢ

"The Tyrea was an elemental. The strongest ever known with the power to pull together all the forces of the elements with just a thought."

Carmella tried to ignore him hours later, but there was no stopping the sound of his voice. "Tyre could control the minds of men, with the secondary elemental powers as well as disarming talents. He was the most powerful man to ever live. So far, of all the little bastards he planted behind the Tyrea's back, only a few have been blessed with both power and honor. We couldn't take the chance that you were one of the few."

As an explanation, it sucked. He had played her. Every moment they had been together he had been lying to her, drawing her in, easing her, reassuring her until the moment her soul accepted what her mind didn't want to see, and opened for him. Love. She had fallen in love with him in one blinding instant, and in the next everything inside her had shattered.

Her insides felt raw, ripped away by the stark, blinding truth of what she had seen in his heart and the pain of knowing it existed. God, had she ever hurt so badly in her life? Had she ever known such desolation within her own soul? Even as the rage had built inside her, the flames erupting from her hands, she had pulled back on the power, trying to control it, to extinguish it. Even though a part of her relished the overriding satisfaction of knowing that at least for an instant, she had caused him pain as well.

"I'm not in the mood for a history lesson, Ryder. This has nothing to do with Tyre and everything to do with you being a jackass. Get over it. I will."

She wouldn't look at him as he drove the vehicle, concentrating instead on the visual display screen as she anticipated facing Torren as well. She had glimpsed his expression earlier. His face was lined, heavy with regret as he watched her. But she knew he didn't regret his actions. It was what she had done that he regretted. What he had seen inside her soul that ate at him. What had he seen that would make him lock her in invisible chains, make him watch her with such anger?

She wouldn't cry, she promised herself as she stared back at him. She would not let him see the tears that were damned near choking her right now. Her stomach was roiling with the pain, her heart ready to explode with it. Son of a bitch, it was just her luck to fall in love with a PSI agent. She thought she was smarter than that; thought her powers would be enough to protect her. She had been wrong.

It was the curse of Fyrebrands. Of the few documented, each had told of the moment their lovers had touched their souls. There were no secrets, no apprehensions between such couples. They were bonded.

It was said it had been the way of Tyre and the Tyrea. That before Tyre convinced himself he was a god, he had first been a man, and his soul had touched the Tyrea's. Carmella's great-grandmother. But even as great as that love had been, it had done nothing to stem the evil inside Tyre.

"I wasn't a jackass, Carmella," he growled. Satisfaction surged through her as she heard the anger growing in his voice. "I let you see the truth. You chose to overlook my feelings for you. All you could see was the deceit."

"Are you fucking crazy?" It was a rhetorical question. Of course he was crazy, he was demonstrating that now. "You think this is about your job with PSI? Do you think I was so stupid that I didn't already suspect, Ryder? Do you think you're the only PSI agent to have ever come after me?"

He lowered his brows into a brooding frown, a question in his eyes that he refused to voice. She smiled slowly, mockingly, as she watched his jaw bunch with fury.

He, of course, wanted to know if she had fucked any of the agents sent out after her. Let him wonder. The mental exercise would do him good.

"You're a descendent of Tyre Leyton and his lover, the Tyrea," he said softly. "You couldn't be trusted without testing, Carmella."

"And did I pass your little test, Ryder?" she asked him softly. "When I let you into my soul did you see the monster you expected to see?"

He didn't show surprise, but he would be too good for that. At least he was now aware that she knew how he saw her. A monster. There, lurking behind his deceit, what he thought was his love for her, had been the twisting, deformed image he thought resided inside her. The image of what he expected to see, even after she had opened herself to him, had nearly destroyed her. He had never believed in her, not completely. He had never thought she was honorable or innocent of Tyre's crimes, and she feared, after seeing the strength of that shadow, that he never would.

"I never thought you were a monster, Carmella." He shook his head, though he avoided her gaze.

She wedged herself uncomfortably into the corner of the seat watching him, her insides burning with pain as she tried to come to grips with everything she had lost in the space of a few, fragile seconds.

"You're such a self-righteous bastard. You and Torren both," she breathed out, resigned. "Have you managed to convince yourself that I deserve to die now? Another monster put away, isn't that how it works, Ryder?"

"Goddammit, Carmella, where do you come up with this crap?" He was fuming, watching her with such brooding anger that it set off a firestorm of fury inside her. He had no right to be furious with her. No right to hold her in chains or in shields. She hadn't lied to him. He had lied to her.

"How did it feel fucking a monster, Ryder?" she snarled, baring her teeth as she fought her pain. "Was the novelty worth it? Do we fuck different than normal women?"

She could feel Torren's presence strengthening around her and fought to keep a shield between her and the man she had once welcomed into her heart and her mind. He had lied to her as well, and she couldn't forget it.

"I won't continue this argument with you." Ryder shook his head, his expression troubled. She liked that. Liked seeing the sudden, internal conflict in his gaze.

"What argument, Ryder? Am I proclaiming my innocence? I want to cut your fucking heart from your chest, I'm not denying it."

"Stop it, Carmella." He breathed in heavily.

"Do you think these chains will stop me, Ryder?" She lifted her hands, the invisible bands of energy cutting a wound in her soul that she feared would never heal. "Do you think you're not the first bastard to try to restrain me?"

"Dammit, Carmella, I just want you to cool off," he snapped. "You're in no frame of mind to follow me and most likely more than capable of attacking. Give yourself time to cool off."

"You son of a bitch, you put me in chains," she screamed, her fury overwhelming her. "You fucking lied to me and on top of it all you didn't even have the decency to try to believe in me. And you expect me not to be angry?"

"You washed my fucking back in flames, Carmella," he yelled back at her. "I'm not in the mood to be roasted tonight, baby."

"You deserved it." She moved forward until they were nearly nose-to-nose. "And don't fool yourself, moron. If I wanted you roasted you would be toast now, not sitting there with the little added power you managed to absorb. You were just waiting on an excuse, just waiting to lock me down and to convince yourself how dangerous I was. The blood of Tyre," she snarled. "A monster, just like he was."

She watched his face closely, his gaze becoming cool, shuttered.

"Get some rest." His voice was perfectly pitched, even and firm. "We have a long ride ahead of us."

Carmella threw herself back in the seat, staring at him with a sneer on her lips. "You won't keep me restrained much longer, Ryder."

"You're disarmed for the moment, Carmella. Try using your powers and you'll only hurt yourself."

She smiled. A tight sarcastic curve of her lips that she noticed had him frowning in suspicion. "I have never depended solely on my powers, Ryder. I will get out of these chains, and when I do, you will never get the chance to get them back on me."

He stared at her for a long, tense moment before he sighed deeply and turned away from her. Carmella drew in a hard breath as she pushed back the pain, the tears. It didn't help to cry. Tears solved nothing. She laid her head against the side of the Hummer and closed her eyes.

Ryder's shield was reinforced with her own. She wasn't powerless, no matter what he thought. He was stronger; she had no doubt. His disarming abilities gave him an edge she couldn't fight with her gifts, but there were times when stealth and cunning far exceeded physical power. Times when a woman just had to show a man how stupid he was, whether she enjoyed the exercise or not. Ryder was about to learn.

\* \* \* \* \*

*Fix it. Or else.* Ryder breathed in deeply as Torren's thoughts smacked into his brain with the force of a fist against his head. He nearly swayed with the pain and the shock of having his shield overtaken so easily. He was stronger than Ryder had thought.

Bad move, Torren. Never show your greatest strength. Remember? Torren had pounded it into his brain years before.

*Let me past that shield, Ryder. You're killing her.* Fury, a friend's pain, it all echoed in the thought.

Ryder glanced back at Carmella again. She looked so small, huddled in the corner of the seat, her eyes closed, her face pale.

I'm not controlling that shield, Torren. He ached with that knowledge. The only shield I have around her is the one controlling her powers. Carmella is blocking herself.

Torren's shock, his worry, filled Ryder's brain. Ryder could feel the other man gathering his strength, and sending himself back toward Carmella. Psychic frustration filled the interior of the Hummer.

Goddammit! I warned you. Torren's thought was cold, bitter. What the hell did you do to her, Ryder? What did she see in your soul?

Ryder frowned. Love. His deception. What more could she have seen?

There had to be more. Torren's force was nearly demonic in its anger, its fear. She's known deception before. She would have seen the truth of your heart, whatever it was. What was it?

You're making excuses for her, Torren. His own thoughts were bleak. She struck out in anger alone. Because I deceived her. Because you did. She released her power because of that anger, just as Tyre did. The world had yet to heal from that wound.

There was silence. A complete numbing silence as he felt Torren stepping out of his thoughts slowly, shock resounding around him. What had he said to so surprise the man who had once sworn he could never be surprised?

*You're a fool.* Torren was in no way pleased. Not that Ryder cared, but still… *Now fix it. Fix it, or you'll deal with me.*

The other man was gone as quickly as he had invaded Ryder's mind. He sighed deeply, tiredly. He'd be damned if he knew what to do now.

Fix it, he grunted silently. Torren was strong…stronger perhaps than Ryder had suspected. But no amount of strength could just fix this.

# Chapter Seventeen

ഇ

They arrived at Torren's location two days later. The beach house was sheltered behind large dunes and swaying palms, its weathered outer planks bleached by salt and wind.

The sturdy, one-story house looked inviting, comfortable, but Carmella was not relaxed. The Hummer came to a stop outside the opened front door as Ryder turned from her, his gaze going to her wrists and ankles. A surge of power enfolded the invisible shackles and within seconds they had fallen to the floor.

Time's almost up, she thought to herself a bit sadly as Ryder exited the vehicle before opening the door for her to step out as well.

"Torren's here?" The shield she had placed around herself kept her from sensing the psychic path she often used with her commander.

"Come in and find out." He gripped her arm as he led her into the beach house.

And there stood Torren. Just inside the large living room, watching their entrance with hooded hazel eyes. His expression was as calm and tranquil as she had ever seen it, but she knew those eyes. He was seething with anger. With her, or with Ryder?

"Try both," he answered her silent thought with a whiplash of harsh fury.

And she didn't really give a damn. He was as handsome as ever. His flowing, dark brown hair rippling to the middle of his shoulders, his hard muscular body standing straight and tall, as perfect and confident as always. Seeing it—seeing him—only made the fury burn hotter inside her.

She stalked across the room, and came face to face with the man who had saved her life and her soul more than once.

She smiled up at him, baring her teeth as he frowned. Before he could flinch she had clenched her fist and drove it with all her remaining strength into the side of his face.

Torren stumbled back, his eyes rounding first in surprise then narrowing furiously as he stared down at her.

"I deserved that," he growled. "But you deserve this."

Before she could evade him, one hand locked in her hair, the other at her hip as he jerked her to him, his lips grinding down on hers. Carmella could only whimper as she struggled against him. His tongue plunged into her mouth, staking his claim on her senses and her mind as he held her tight against his hard body.

The length of his cock seared her through the confining shields of their clothing. His hard hands were a brand at her hip and her head, his passion a blazing conqueror as he tried to possess her soul with the kiss.

Carmella quaked inside. She thought she could resist him. Thought her love for Ryder would make her immune. Unfortunately, in that instant, she realized that Torren, too, had the key to her soul. He always had.

She whimpered in distress. There was no escape. Her hands tightened on his shoulders as she fought the response she was giving him. She was trapped between the two men, heart, body and soul.

"Not trapped, Carmella. Protected. Always protected." Ryder whispered at her back, his hands smoothing along the curves of her rear as his lips stroked over her bare shoulder.

Protected? They had betrayed her. Never trusted her. She moaned into the kiss, fighting them and herself as emotion and sensation overwhelmed her.

She had fought for so long. Fighting was a necessary part of her, but in this instance, her body refused to draw the necessary strength to do anything but revel in each caress it was being given.

Finally, when she thought she would pass out from the fiery heat running rampant between the three of them, Torren lifted his head. He stared down at her, his eyes dark, his expression carnal.

"Now, we can talk. You hit me again, Carmella, and I'll paddle your ass."

Carmella jerked away from the two of them, stalking to the other side of the room before she turned back to face them.

"What is this fascination you two have with spanking me?"

She didn't like the sudden dark intensity that swept over their expressions.

"Oh, you'd like it. Eventually," Ryder promised her, his smile a bit too ruthless to suit her.

She snarled back at him. "Don't bet on getting the chance to try it. I've had my fill of lies from both of you. Now tell me what the hell is going on here or I'm gone."

She watched them, amazed at the differences between the two men, and yet, how much they were alike. Carmella blinked, suddenly realizing how much she cared for each man. How much she loved them, both.

Torren, for obvious reasons. They had been lovers as well as friends. He had covered her back, protected her, helped her survive. Ryder had just taken her over. Her heart had given her no choice when he had shown her both the dominance and the gentleness he held for her. But he didn't trust her. Torren couldn't trust her. Not really. Not if he had set this plan up to begin with.

"Carmella." Torren breathed in deeply. "I know you're angry. Very angry. And I know little of this is making sense to you right now."

"Now there's an understatement," she snapped as she crossed her arms over her breasts.

"Do you trust me, Carmella?" he asked her, his voice soft, reflective.

Did she? She stared back at him, seeing the softness in his hazel eyes, seeing the man she had loved, in so many ways, for so long.

"You know I do, Torren. I wouldn't be here if I didn't." She would have run as hard and as fast as her legs would have carried her the moment she realized Ryder was a PSI agent if she hadn't trusted him.

Ryder crossed his arms over his chest as he watched them, his gaze soft. She didn't want him soft. She wanted him angry. She wanted them all angry so she could rid herself of the fury rushing through her.

"How far do you trust me?" Torren asked her.

Carmella could feel her heart speeding up in her chest at his tone of voice. It was hot, sexual. A tone he had used only rarely with her, even while they had been lovers.

She swallowed tightly, her gaze swinging between the two of them. Torren and Ryder both would be aware of her conflicting emotions right now. Her inability to decide which man held more of her heart. Which she could bear letting go? From the looks of them, neither intended to let her go.

"Right now, only about as far as I can see you," she snorted. "Either of you, if you want the truth."

"You know I've studied the advanced psychic phenomena," Torren told her softly. "The old records, and many of my own suspicions."

She nodded slowly. She was well aware of that.

"Fyrebrands are often unique in many ways." He shrugged. "Their passions are hotter, more tempestuous, requiring a greater amount of control from the person possessing them."

"I'm aware of your theories, Torren." She had never bothered to worry overmuch about them until now.

"The personal control eventually weakens a person without an outlet. It breaks down. It breeds a loss of emotion, a loss of joy." He speared her with a hard, intense look. "I've noticed both in you."

"I'm loyal." She braced herself for whatever came next. "You've never had reason to question that, Torren."

"And I don't question it now." Command, stern and unflinching, filled his voice. "Your soul touched Ryder's, but you held back. Just as you did with me before all this began. You kept your control rather than giving it to him. That was what caused the shadows of distrust that you saw."

She shot Ryder a hateful look. "What have you convinced him of?" she snapped furiously. "You didn't trust me."

"You didn't trust me." He shrugged lazily. "If you had, you would have first, been honest with me. Second, you would not have shadowed that inner part of yourself, Carmella. The part that reveals everything you are."

She was breathing hard and fast now, looking between the two men who each held a part of her soul. Both men too handsome, too damned sexual. Being caught between them, even like this, was too intense for her to handle.

"I'm not one of your experiments." She turned on Torren then, knowledge flooding her mind. They wanted her to feel helpless. Caught between them. Controlled. Bound to them both.

"Unfortunately, you are." Ryder's voice was a rough, sexual caress across her nerve endings. "Your life depends on it, Carmella. I won't let you throw it away because of stubbornness."

She fought to still her breathing, to control the anger beginning to flood her.

"And exactly how does my life depend on whatever the hell you two are hatching up?" She looked from one to the other, seeing more than just concern, more than just desire.

"When you go in with us for testing at PSI headquarters, Carmella, there will be no hiding who and what you are. Without evidence of control, you'll be signing your own death sentence. You know that."

She fought the tremble that threatened to shake her body. "Then I won't go in. I have no intention of going in." She turned to Torren, trembling now as she saw the truth on his face. "What have you done, Torren?"

"Wrong." Ryder's voice rose at her declaration. "You're mine too, Carmella. Mine and Torren's. You know it, and I know it. I won't let you take the easy way out on this. Goddammit it. PSI headquarters sent me out to look for you. They know you exist."

She could feel the blood draining from her face. They knew who she was. They knew where she was. How? Could they be right about her shields, her controls? Or had Torren betrayed her? She watched him, felt him, but couldn't believe he would do so.

"Ryder can disarm you, as you've seen, and what powers he can't absorb, I can. But if you give up control, together we can amplify those powers as well as still the unprovoked anger that sometimes fills you, Carmella. But we can't do that unless you open to us completely. You have to open to us willingly."

*Us?* She screamed the thought at Torren. Her gaze swung between the two men, realizing…knowing, that neither man planned to let her go. She wouldn't be a lover to one; she would love two.

*Us, Carmella.* Ryder's response was a sensual caress through her mind, leaving her trembling in the aftermath.

"How?" She ran her fingers through her hair in desperation. "For God's sake, Torren. He has never trusted me. Ever."

"Because you haven't let him in. You haven't truly let either of us in," Torren snapped. "You are not normal, Carmella, no matter how much you wish you were. Neither

114

are we. The very talents that make you different make your emotional processes more difficult. We will complete you. To do that, we need you just as you need us. Ryder opened himself completely to you, just as I did. It's the reason you can feel my honesty and see his suspicions, otherwise you would have never seen those shadows, which rose when you blocked him."

"No..." It couldn't be that easy.

"I was there!" Torren yelled back at her, furious now. "Do you understand me, Carmella? I was there. Do you think I would have trusted your mind to anyone without observing it? Do you actually believe I wasn't there when you gave him the last part of heart that I could never seem to hold?"

Her eyes widened, equal parts fury and arousal filling her in one blinding instant. He had been there? Watching? In her mind... She swallowed tightly, her gaze moving slowly to Ryder. She had fought to keep Torren blocked during their trip to his location. Had fought to try to make sense of her needs for both men, when she knew — or thought she knew — she could have only one.

"You're too complacent," Ryder told her softly. "You aren't blocking nearly as well as you should, and you're getting careless. Your frustration level is too high, Carmella. It affects your objectivity and your performance. It's too high, because you refuse to submit to what you know you want."

She laughed. She couldn't help it. In their faces, more amused than really offended, she laughed at both of them. They intended to share her. There had never been a danger of losing either man. The whole elaborate plot was to cement Ryder's hold on her before they slapped her with the truth.

"You're joking? Right? You're turning this into something sexual. Something that you can so obviously help me with," she sneered. "What do you have in mind, Ryder? Double-teaming me? Let's see, I've already fucked Torren." She shot him a distasteful look. "Not that it ever did me much good. And I'm not real pleased with you at the moment, either."

"Didn't do you much good?" Torren kept his voice soft, a warning in and of itself. "Carmella, it's not like you to lie, baby. You forget; I'm a seer, among other things. I knew what was coming. I knew who was coming. I wasn't about to screw it up by giving you the illusion that you could get anywhere else, what you will only get one way."

Carmella bit her lip. She didn't like the sharp contraction that fisted her womb as he spoke. She sure as hell didn't like the way her juices seemed to flood her pussy.

She turned to Ryder as he moved, walking to her slowly, his expression filled with determination.

"You said you loved me," she whispered. "This isn't love. From either of you."

"Isn't it?" His expression turned immeasurably gentle as he reached her, his hand rising to touch her face. "Does love have a definition, Carmella? Isn't it acceptance, complete acceptance of the one you love? Complete protection and the fulfillment of their needs? No matter those needs? You need what we have to offer. Not just for yourself, but for us as well."

# Chapter Eighteen

Carmella fought to breathe just as hard as she fought the heat tingling under her skin. Her muscles tightened as the sensations gathered in the pit of her stomach, working their way over her body.

She looked at Torren, seeing the heat in his gaze, the affection, his concern.

"You don't love me." She shook her head as she turned back to Ryder. "Neither of you can possibly love me. This doesn't make sense."

Confusion didn't sit well with her. The morass of longings, fantasies and desires that had always tormented her had been something she had never thought to actually experience. She could have, at any given time, but her fear of allowing herself that greatest fantasy had always held her back. Now, faced with the only two men she had ever cared for, Carmella was terrified.

"Carmella, I love you beyond life. I did months ago, when I first touched your mind, first entered your fantasies. In all those fantasies, Torren lingered just out of view. You didn't even realize yourself what you were doing. For a while, I didn't realize what you needed."

She shook her head desperately, fighting him, fighting herself. She flinched as Torren came closer. His eyes, usually a cool, tranquil hazel, now glittered with darker highlights as he watched her.

"He holds your woman's soul," he whispered as Ryder's hands moved to the hem of her blouse. "But you and I both know, Carmella, that I too hold a part of your heart."

"No." She wanted to jerk away from them as she felt the heat intensifying under her skin. "You don't understand. It was a just fantasy."

Her nipples were so hard, so filled with longing, she felt as though they would burst as the cloth of her shirt raked over them. Torren gripped her wrists, raising them a second before his mouth covered one swollen peak.

"Oh God." Her knees weakened. Her gaze flew to Ryder. He pulled the shirt up her arms, his hand gripping her wrists as Torren released them. All the while, he watched the other man suckle the smooth, supple flesh.

His eyes darkened in arousal and when he looked at her, they were filled with approval.

"Every Fyrebrand has her weakness," he whispered as he dropped her shirt to the floor. "This is yours, Carmella. And I give it to you, whenever you want it, however you want it."

As he finished speaking, Torren gripped her nipple between his teeth, exerting just enough pressure to leave her gasping on the edge of pain as his tongue flicked over the little tip with sensuous delight. Carmella's eyes widened at the sensations, a breathless scream issuing from her throat as her body jerked, shuddered in the embrace of the two men.

"Easy, Carmella." Ryder's lips brushed hers, the warm rasp of his beard causing her to whimper at the added sensation. "I want you to let go. Just let go. Let me and Torren take care of you, baby. It's okay."

Carmella shook her head, though she couldn't control her gasp as Torren began to suckle greedily at her flesh once more. She had to have control. She couldn't lose it. She couldn't take the chance. To relinquish it to either of them meant the power surging through her body—flames erupting, scorching her—would then be their responsibility to tame. Her control, her need to control, was too much a part of her.

"Please, Ryder." Tears welled in her eyes as she stared back at him. "I can't do this."

"You don't have a choice." For all its gentleness, his voice was firm. "When I return to the agency with you, Carmella, there will be no doubt in anyone's mind that you have bonded with both of us. That your powers are controlled. That I control that part of you. That you are no danger to them or to anyone else. I will not risk your life."

He didn't give her time to answer. He took her lips in a kiss that effectively stilled any other argument. Not that she would have argued further. Torren's hands were pushing the waistband of her pants over her hips, Ryder's tongue was devouring hers, and all Carmella could do was hold on and pray she could at least hold a measure of her restraint close. Dear God, she didn't want to hurt them.

She had already burned Ryder in her fury. What was she capable of with no control whatsoever?

"Shush your fears, baby," Ryder whispered against her lips. "I'll take care of you this time. I promise. Just trust me. Me and Torren. We won't let anything happen."

Cool air chilled her tender nipple as Torren released it, moving back as Ryder picked her up in his arms. Carmella held onto him, caught in the dizzying knowledge of what was to come. Torren knew her powers. He wouldn't falter. Surely he wouldn't. He never had. And Ryder knew the damage she could cause. He could disarm her. He could keep her from hurting any of them. Couldn't he?

She whimpered as they laid her on the bed, quickly removing her boots and her clothing before removing their own. Her head was whirling with the knowledge of what was coming. Fears and desires, fantasies and reality, collided with such chaos that she couldn't seem to find an anchor to hold her tumultuous emotions stable.

She could feel her flesh prickling with power, heating her, intensifying the sensations of Ryder and Torren's hands smoothing over her body. Ryder came up beside her, one arm going under her shoulders as he lifted her into his embrace.

"I'm just going to hold you, baby," he whispered at her ear as he reclined against the headboard, pulling Carmella against his chest as Torren eased her legs apart. "Just hold you, and show you that you have nothing to fear."

Nothing to fear? She could feel the lust scorching her insides, flooding her pussy. It was all she could do to hold back her cries as she watched Torren lower himself between her thighs while he gazed at her cunt in hungry fascination. Torren loved driving her insane with his mouth when they had been lovers. She could have handled it. She had before. But before, she hadn't had Ryder's back bracing hers, his hands cupping her breasts, his fingers tweaking her nipples as he whispered encouragement in her ear.

"Easy, baby," Ryder soothed her as Torren pushed his hands under her rear, lifting her to his mouth. "Slow and easy. You like that, don't you?"

His fingers tightened on the hard points of her breasts as Torren's tongue distended and began a slow, lazy swipe up her soaking slit.

She felt her scalp prickle in warning. The flames were building in her mind, terrifying her.

"No. No, please…" She thrashed her head against Ryder's chest, fighting it, terrified of the consequences.

"Trust me, Carmella," Ryder whispered at her ear. "You have to trust me, baby. Let me have the heat. I can take it. Give it to me, Carma."

Torren's lips covered her clit, his tongue stroking around it, never touching it, causing it to swell further as the pressure echoed through her body. Each caress felt deliberately timed, slow and intense, provoking the ultimate pleasure.

Carmella tightened fighting the sensations, the pleasure. She had never given control of herself or her powers to another living person. To do so now terrified her. They could use her. Could destroy her.

"Carmella." Ryder's voice was stern, the sound of it causing her pussy to clench in need.

Torren moved one hand from beneath her buttocks, sliding slowly along her flesh until it stopped between her thighs. She shuddered.

"Torren... Please..." She was panting now, a fine film of perspiration coating her body as she felt his fingers stop at the entrance to her greedy cunt. "Torren, I can't do this..."

He moaned against her clit. Carmella couldn't stop the strangled scream that escaped her throat as she arched closer to his mouth. Oh God, it was too good. He was destroying her with his touch. She lowered her hands, trying to push him away, only to have Ryder catch her wrists again and stretch them behind her head as he moved her quickly.

Before she could do more than cry out, he had her on her knees as Torren turned on his back, pushing her thighs wide, his tongue spearing hard and fast inside the soaked depths of her cunt. Pleasure spasmed through her womb, raced through her bloodstream.

Torren's body was stretched out before her as Ryder knelt beside her, holding her arms behind her back, staring down at her with an expression of savage sensuality.

She struggled against his grip, then screamed out as Torren's hand landed heavily on her buttock. Her entire body stilled an instant before she felt the flames beginning to rise from her skin.

"God, no!" she screamed out, trying to move away from Ryder, terrified of what would happen now.

Torren wouldn't stop, wouldn't allow her to control her response. He slapped her ass again, then did the unthinkable. His fingers parted the cheeks of her rear, one running down the cleft until it speared the tiny little hole waiting below. His finger slid in deep, hard, pushing through the sensitive tissue, stretching her, opening her.

"Torren." She tried to scream his name, but her wail was one of such pleasure it shocked her own ears.

Torren's tongue was a demon of lust. Spearing into her sensitive cunt, thrusting through the thick juices, lapping at her greedily as he slid his finger easily into her back hole.

"Beautiful, baby." Ryder held her steady as his head lowered to lap at her nipples. His teeth raked them, his lips covered them, suckling deeply as Torren continued to fuck her tormented pussy with his wicked tongue.

She was shaking, sweat dripping from her body, as she held onto her control with the thinnest of threads.

"Let go, Carmella," Ryder whispered from her breast. "Give it to me, baby. Let go."

She shook her head, gasping for breath. A hand landed on her buttock again. She wasn't certain whose. The little sting only deepened the pleasure of Torren's tongue thrusting rapidly into her spasming pussy, and Ryder's little nips at her sensitive nipples.

She couldn't hold on. She knew she couldn't.

When she felt them moving her again, she could only whimper, her body following their commands easily as her mind scrambled for balance. There was none. Before she could do more than scream his name, Ryder had stretched out on the bed as Torren moved up beside her, helping her to straddle the other man's body. Carmella stared into his dark eyes as he held her hips down, encouraging her darkly as Ryder's cock began to sink slowly into the tormented depths of her cunt.

"Torren, please…" Her voice was a ragged plea as her body began to greedily suck Ryder's thick cock into it. "I'm scared."

Her head was resting on Torren's chest as he knelt beside her, his arms supporting her as Ryder began to work his erection inside her. Too much. Too good. She was crying, tears falling slowly down her cheeks as the pleasure became unbearable and the heat inside her began rising once again.

"You're so tight," Torren whispered in her ear. "I remember how tight your sweet pussy is, Carmella. I know how he's stretching it. How good it's making you feel. When he's in—all the way in—your sweet cunt gloving every inch of his cock, I'm going to take your ass. I'm going to take it, Carmella, and you're going to love it."

Torren's hand slid down her back, his finger sliding inside the little hole once again as Ryder groaned out beneath her. She bucked, driving Ryder further inside her as she fought for more of the hot pressure from Torren's finger.

It was too much. She needed it too much. She bent over Ryder's body, going into the arms that opened for her, then enfolded her, screaming out against Ryder's chest as his cock and Torren's finger stole her sanity. She was lost. Adrift. She could do nothing now but trust them to do what was best. To protect her and themselves.

She was only vaguely aware of Torren moving. The feel of cool lubricating gel being worked inside her anus. Long, broad fingers stretching her, preparing her, as Ryder lodged every inch of his cock deep inside her.

Carmella whimpered, awaiting the final invasion. The ecstatic pain she knew would be more than her mind could control. She turned her head on Ryder's shoulder, her tears wetting his flesh.

"Please," she whispered as she felt Torren move behind her, the head of his cock pressing against her rear entrance. "Please, don't let me hurt you."

In that second she lost her breath, and her control. Torren gave little concession to her anal virginity or her fears. With steady, intense pressure he began to ease the thick length of his cock into the ultra tight entrance, his fingers spreading her rear cheeks apart, his groan echoing around her.

It was pleasure and pain. Heated rapturous agony. An inferno.

As Carmella felt Torren's cock slide inside her in a stroke of lightning-hot pleasure, she lost the last remaining shreds of control. She was a vessel now. Pleasure so rich and intense it bordered on pain. Impaled, penetrated, taken. She felt her soul splinter and images she could have never imagined began to ripple through her as Ryder and Torren began to move inside her with deep, powerful strokes. Torren laughing with her as he fucked her during the months they were lovers. She saw his laughter but felt his sadness. She was partly his, partly another's. Without Ryder, without his natural balance, his ability to make her love, none of them had truly been whole.

He completed the circle they were meant to be. Ryder, watching her from afar, impatience and fear driving him as he dreamed of her, searched for her, felt her anger and her grief until the moment he saw her picture in a file. Then he knew her. All of her. Ached for her.

Power swirled around her, through her, inside her, until it erupted, as she had always feared it would. They held her tight, fucking into her, driving her insane with the pleasure until it exploded. She exploded. Heart, body, mind and soul. The orgasm that swept through her entered the soul of each man, just as they, too, reached the fiery peak of their releases.

Hot blasts of semen poured into her body as flames tickled along her flesh, only to be absorbed by the two men. Pleasure speared through her pussy, her womb, stealing her breath, her silent screams a mere breath of sound as she flew from her own body and mingled with the souls of the men who had finally pierced the boundaries of her power. Completed.

Darkness swirled around her then as the violence of her release stole her awareness. She could feel the ripples surging through her body, the power pouring from her mind, only to be absorbed by the men sheltering her. With it the last of the dark restlessness that haunted her evaporated, and she felt the peace that began to take its place.

Carmella came to long seconds later; held between Ryder and Torren as they gasped for breath, sweat dripping from their bodies as Torren finally eased his cock from the tight grip of her anus. Ryder was still buried inside her, though the steel-hard insistence of his erection had eased somewhat. His hand clasped her head to his chest, his lips whispered over her ear, her cheek.

"We love you, Carmella. We both love you," he told her, his voice tender, immeasurably soft. "We're bound now, always."

And they were. He eased her to his side, sighing deeply as drowsiness began to overtake them all. Clasped to Ryder's chest, Torren warming her back, she was protected. Safe. For the first time in all the years she could remember, Carmella slept easily, at peace.

# Epilogue

**ဆ**

Shannon Reidel stared at the closed file on her desk, smoothing her hand over each one, a sense of accomplishment filling her. Three down. So many more to go. The stamp on the outside of the files proclaimed them completed. Inside, the final tests on the three women were evaluated, notated and determined as a "Safe Risk".

She thought of the three woman and the agents she had sent after them. Testing hadn't been easy on them. It was exhausting, but they had come through it perfectly. And happily.

They were beautiful young women. Each possessing characteristics so reminiscent of their mother that it was heart-breaking. Their reunion had been joyous. They had been filled with laughter, with tears and joy, as they all embraced beneath the protective regard of the men who accompanied them. Men who loved them, completed them, eased them.

The three women, direct descendents of the two most powerful psychics the world had ever known, were safe. But they weren't the last of Tyre's seed. There were others.

She pulled the files across the desk, her hand laying on each, pausing for long seconds as she closed her eyes and breathed in deeply. So many were out there. So many of the children had already perished. Fine, honorable men and women who had been bequeathed the power of Tyre, without the cerebral damage he had incurred during the experiments to advance his powers.

So long ago. So long. She lowered her head, shaking it, her chest aching with her pain.

He had been a good man once. Long, long ago. Before the experiments. Before he had been driven insane by his own power, his own fears. Before he had been taken from her.

She rose to her feet, walking slowly to the small bathroom off her office to the mirror above the sink. She touched her face. It was still unlined. Still as perfect as it had been the day she had walked away from the man who held her soul.

Her eyes were still clear, her body perfectly toned. For nearly a century and a half in age, she looked damned good. She tilted her head, wondering if the scientists who tried to rate her powers, who tried to tamper with them, could have ever envisioned what they created. There wasn't a gray hair on her head. Nothing to indicate she was more than the thirty years of age her file proclaimed.

The Tyrea.

She gripped the sink tightly. Tyre. Dear God, how long and empty the years had been without him. How desolate her life had been, until she had come up with a way to heal in part, the wounds he had created.

Sweet Tyre, she thought, how I miss you.

She lowered her head, remembering his kisses, so bold and dominant, his touch firing every cell in her body to life as their souls mingled. The gift and the curse of an elemental whose main power was that of fire. A Fyrebrand.

But it had all been over so quickly. Her fists clenched as she fought back her tears. Tears were for the deepest part of the night. The long black hours when she had nothing else to do but to remember. His touch. The sound of his voice. The curve of his cheek. And she had never forgotten a moment, a touch.

She breathed in hard and deep, staring back into the office, thinking of the lives that had yet to be saved. And those that would be lost. So many innocent lives. So much left to accomplish. And it was her payment. Her atonement. Her curse for ever convincing the man she loved that such power could be controlled. That the experiments could aid the world. Her fault. On her shoulders lay the near destruction of the world, and now on her shoulders lay the reparation of it. It had begun with these three. But it would be a long time before she would see the end.

# SURRENDER

# Dedication

ℰℛ

*My sister Lue Anne, who's always there, no matter what.*
*Thanks, Sis. You make life easier when it gets really hard.*

# Chapter One

ഇ

"Tess, you coming to my party?" It was her father's voice on her answering machine that finally roused her from sleep. "You better be here, girl. I'm tired of you staying away. You call me back."

The line disconnected. Tess sighed as she opened her eyes. She would have preferred the dream to the stark loneliness that awaited her when she opened her eyes. At least there, even in the dark, frightening abyss of desires too dark to name, she had a purpose, rather than her fears.

She stared down at the large stuffed gorilla she clutched to her chest in her sleep. A present from her father when she left with her mother. Something to keep the bad dreams away, he had said sadly, even though she had been an adult. Tess often had bad dreams.

Perhaps she shouldn't have left as well, Tess often thought. She was just entering college at the time, and could have made her own choice. But her mother had needed her. Or Tess had thought she did. Now she wasn't certain if her mother needed her, or merely needed to control her.

"Tess, you awake now?" Her mother, Ella James called from the bottom of the downstairs hallway, her voice barely penetrating the distance.

Tess had installed her own phone line straight out of college and moved her bedroom to the upper floor where her mother rarely ventured. She needed her privacy, and her mother was prone to butt in wherever she could. The stairs kept her from venturing into Tess's privacy very often.

"Yeah, Mom. I'm awake," she yelled back, rising from bed, imagining her mother's moue of distaste. It was Saturday, for God's sake. She was entitled to sleep in. She could just imagine her mother's expression if she knew it was her father's call that woke her.

Resigned, Tess got of bed and headed for the shower.

Tess was well aware of her mother's disgust for her father's lifestyle. Jason Delacourte didn't stay home or keep regular hours or play the nine to five game. He owned a national electronics corporation and lived the lifestyle he chose. He gave dinners, attended charities and threw yearly parties. Ella preferred her books and her quiet and anything that didn't involve a man. She had done her best to raise her daughter the same way.

Tess did hate parties. She always had and she knew she always would. She invariably ended up going alone. Always ended up leaving alone. Parties jinxed her. Men jinxed her, they had for years. But she was committed to this party. She had promised. What could she do but get ready to go?

She grimaced, confused as she pondered her lack of a love life. Or perhaps sex life. She wasn't a great believer in love or the happily ever after stuff. She had rarely seen it work, her own parents were an example of that one. And her father's second marriage seemed more rocky than solid.

She frowned as she usually did when she thought of her father's new wife. Well, perhaps not new. Jason Delacourte, her father, had been married for nearly three years now to Melissa. The woman still insisted that everyone call her Missy. As though she were still a teenager. Tess snarled with distaste. Of course, the woman was barely thirty-five, ten years younger than her father, and nearly ten years older then Tess. The least he could have done, she sniped silently, was marry a woman closer to his own age.

She could barely tolerate being in the same room with 'Missy'. The woman gave dumb blonde a new meaning. How she managed to be related to a man touted as a genius, Tess had no idea. But she was. Cole Andrews was Missy's brother, and Tess's father swore Cole had moved Delacourte me to never stop. You're mine Tess, and I know what it takes to give you what you need. When you're ready to accept that, let me know."

Tess shook her head. Wanting it and accepting it were two different things. She had dreamed of it ever since, too humiliated to ask him for it, and he refused to offer a second time.

She touched her smooth, waxed pussy, her eyes closing as she lay back on the bed. The thought of what he wanted terrified her, yet it aroused her to the point of pain. The thought of his cock, so thick and hard, easing into her ass as he penetrated her wet, pleading cunt with a dildo, her tied down, unable to fight, unable to escape whatever he desired, had her soaked with need. He wouldn't hurt her. She knew enough about Cole to know he would never hurt her, but he could show her things she wasn't sure she was ready to know about herself. He could show her a part of herself that she wasn't certain she could handle. That was a frightening thought.

Her fingers eased through the shallow, narrow crease of her cunt, circled her clit. He had promised to eat her there. To run his tongue around her clit, suck it, eat her like honey, a lick at a time. She shuddered, moaning, imagining her finger was his tongue, licking at her cunt, lapping at the slick heat that soaked her pussy. She circled her clit, whispering his name, then moved her fingers back down to the desperate ache in her vagina. She penetrated the tight channel with two of her fingers, biting her lip, wondering how thick and long Cole's fingers would be inside her. He had such a big hands, he would fill her, make her scream for more.

He had whispered the dark promise that he would fuck her ass, take her there, make her scream for him. She bit her lips, her fingers moving, one inserting into that tiny, dark hole while she wished she hadn't packed her vibrator so quickly. As her finger passed the tight entrance, she allowed two fingers of her other hand to sink into her vagina. She could hear his voice in the back of her mind, feel his finger, thicker

Electronics into the financial sphere it now enjoyed as one of the leading electronic manufacturers.

The thought of him caused mixed reactions in Tess, though.

Cole was six feet three inches of hard packed muscle and dark, brooding good looks with a cynical, mocking attitude that drove her crazy. His kisses were the stuff dreams were made of. His fingers were wicked instruments of torturous pleasure; his lips were capable of throwing her into a hypnotic trance when they touched her.

She suppressed a sigh. No man kissed as good as Cole Andrews. It should be a crime that one man should ooze so much sex appeal, and be such an asshole to boot. And it was really a crime that she couldn't get past that one stolen kiss long enough to enjoy any others.

After showering, she quickly blow dried her hair, sighing as she swiped the brush through her shoulder-length black hair one last time before turning back to the open doors of her large closet. She had enough clothes. One thing her father had always done was made certain she was well provided for.

Elementary school teachers didn't make a lot in terms of money, and it wasn't the glamorous job Jason Delacourte had always thought his daughter should hold, but it was what she wanted to do. Besides, it kept her out of the social sphere her stepmother and Cole Andrews moved in. That was a big enough plus to keep her there.

But, she had promised her father she would stay with him for this one week. That she would take the time off work and return to the large family home she had grown up in before his divorce from her mother, and she would try to be his daughter.

It wasn't that she didn't love him, she thought as she packed her suitcase. She did. She loved her father terribly, but Cole was at the house. He stayed there often, and it was Cole she needed to avoid.

After packing the more casual clothes she would need and her treasured, hidden vibrator, Tess moved back to her closet to choose what she would wear for the yearly Valentine's Day party her father gave. It was also the third year anniversary of his marriage to Missy. Yeah, she really wanted to celebrate that one.

She pulled a short, black, silk sheath from the closet and hung it on the doorknob. From her dresser she pulled out a black thong, a lacy matching bra, and smoky silk stockings. The dark colors suited her mood. Valentine's Day was for lovers, and Tess didn't have one. She still didn't understand why she was going to this stupid party.

It wasn't like her father would really miss her. The house would be packed. They didn't need her there. She hadn't attended one of Missy's parties in well over a year now. They were loud, bustling and often turned out a bit too wild for her tastes. Besides, Cole always ended up bringing his latest flame, and pissing her off the first hour into it.

His dark blue eyes would watch her, faintly cynical, always glittering with interest while the bimbos at his side simpered adoringly. She snorted. If she had to simper to hold him, well then—

She sighed desolately. She would probably simper if she thought it would help. If she could learn how. Her mouth always seemed to get the better of her though. His general air of superiority just grated on her. Ever since that first kiss, his hard body holding her captive against the wall as he whispered what he wanted in her ear. Her body had sung in agreement, her mind, shocked and dazed from the images, had kicked in with an instant defense: her smart mouth.

It had been over two years.

She sat down on the bed, still naked, her cunt wet, throbbing at the memory.

"Can you take the heat, baby?" he had whispered to her, holding her against the wall as he ground his cock between her

---

thighs. "I won't lie to you, Tess. I want you bad. But I'm [not] one of your little college boys that you can mess with. I w[ant] you tied to my bed, screaming, begging for me. I wan[t to] pump my dick in that tight little ass of yours, I want to [hear] your cries while I'm buried there and fuck you with a d[ildo] bought just for that tight cunt of yours."

She shook now in remembered arousal and hot despe[rate] need.

"Sure," she had bit out. "And then I can fuck your [ass] next!"

He had had the nerve to laugh at her. Laugh at her as [his] fingers sank into the wet, tight grip of her pussy and [an] orgasm rippled over her body. She'd gasped, feeling the s[oft] heat as it pulsed through her vagina, washing over his fing[ers.] Then he had slid them down to the tight little hole he [had] promised to fuck, one finger sinking in to its first knuc[kle,] sending a flare of pain through her body that she had enjo[yed] too much to be comfortable with.

Tess remembered her fear, throbbing as hot as her l[ust.] She had pushed him away, trembling, unfamiliar with the [hot] pulse of hunger that had flared in her, unlike anything she [had] known before. And he had watched her, his cock a thick, h[ard] outline beneath his pants, his eyes dark as she stood bef[ore] him trembling.

"Pervert!" she had accused him.

His lips had quirked, his eyes flaring in anger.

"And you?" he asked her. "What does that make y[ou,] baby? Because sooner or later, you'll have to admit you w[ant] it."

"What, raped?" she had bit out.

His eyes suddenly softened, a strange smile quirking [his] lips.

"Never rape, Tess. You'll beg me for it. Because we b[oth] know you want it as much as I do. My cock sliding up y[our] tight ass while you scream for me to stop, then screaming

than hers, spearing a dart of pleasurable pain through her as he pierced her ass. And he had told her, warned her he would fuck her there.

Her knees bent, her hips thrusting harder against her own fingers as she imagined Cole between her thighs, licking her, fucking her with his fingers, driving her over the edge as they fucked into her; her cunt, her ass, until —

She cried out as the soft ripples of release washed over her. Her vagina clenched on her fingers, her womb trembling with pleasure. It wasn't the release she had experienced with Cole's fingers or her vibrator, but it took the edge off the lust that seemed to only grow over time.

# Chapter Two

§O

*It wasn't enough. An hour and a cold shower later, Tess's body still simmered with need. Stretched on her bed, her body sheened with sweat as she fought for orgasm, she cursed the phone when it rang at her side. Grimacing when it refused to stop, Tess reached over, grabbing the receiver.*

"Hello." She tried to clear her throat, to still her rapid breaths, and hoped she could explain it away if it was her father. She didn't want him to know his daughter was a raging mass of horny hormones ready to explode.

There was a brief silence, as though the caller were weighing his words.

"Feeling better?" A trace of knowing mockery, a deep, sensually husky voice whispered the words.

Tess flushed at Cole's voice. Damn him.

"I haven't been sick," she bit out, her eyes closing as her vagina pulsed. She smoothed her fingers over her clit, feeling the increased stimulation there. Damn, she could get off with just his voice.

"No, just trying to get off," he said lazily. "I would help. All you have to do is ask."

Ask, ask, her inner voice begged.

"In your dreams." She winced as the words burst from her mouth. Damn him, he put her on the defensive faster than anyone she knew.

"It would appear in yours as well," he said, his mockery suddenly gone. "I know how you sound when you're aroused, Tess. Don't try to lie to me. Let me hear you. Touch yourself for me."

Tess felt her breath strangle in her throat.

"You're a pervert, Cole." She fought for her own control at the sound of that sexy voice. "Isn't phone sex illegal?"

"I'm sure most of what I want to do with you could be termed illegal," he chuckled. "Let's talk about it, Tess. Come on, tell me what you were doing to yourself. Are you using your fingers or a vibrator?"

"I do not have a vibrator." She clenched her teeth over the lie.

"Dildo?" he whispered the words heatedly. "Are you fucking yourself, Tess? Thinking about me, how much I want you?"

"No!" She clenched the receiver in her hand, shaking her head despite the fact that her fingers had returned to her suddenly pulsing cunt.

"I'd like to see you in my bed, Tess, your legs spread, your hands touching your pretty cunt, fucking yourself. Did I ever tell you I bought that dildo I promised you? It's nice and thick, Tess. Almost as large as my cock. I want to watch you use it. See you fuck yourself with it."

"God, Cole," she gasped. "We're on the phone. This is indecent." But her fingers were sinking into her cunt.

"What were you doing before I called, Tess?" His voice was dark, hot. "I know you were touching yourself. I know the sound of your voice when you're ready to come, and you're ready to come, baby."

"No—" She tried to deny the obvious truth, but she couldn't keep her breath from catching as her fingers grazed her clit once again.

"Son of a bitch, Tess," he growled. "Are you close, baby?" His voice deepened. "If I were there, I'd make you scream for it. I'd fuck you so deep and hard you wouldn't be able to stop it. You'd cum for me, Tess. Come for me now, baby. Let me hear you."

139

His voice was so deep, so sensual and aroused it caused her womb to contract almost painfully. Her body bowed, her breath catching on a near sob. He brought all her darkest desires, her deepest fantasies to the forefront of her mind. It terrified her.

"Cole," she whispered his name, wanting to deny him, but her fingers weren't listening as they stroked her clit, sank into her vagina, then moved back to repeat the action.

She was so hot she could barely stand it. So horny she was on the verge of screaming for relief.

"I'm stroking my cock, Tess, listening to you lay there, imagining you touching your juicy cunt, wishing I were with you, watching you fuck yourself with the dildo I bought you." His words caused her to gasp, her womb to contract painfully, her hips to surge into her plunging fingers.

"No." She tossed her head. She couldn't do this.

"Damn, Tess, I want to fuck you," he growled, his voice rough. "I want to be buried so deep and hard inside you you'll never forget it or deny me again. Come for me, damn you. At least let me hear what I can't have. Fuck yourself Tess, give this to me. Those aren't your fingers buried in your pussy, it's my cock. Mine, and I'm going to fuck you until you scream."

Tess's orgasm ripped through her. She shuddered, whimpered, her body tightening to the point of pain before she felt her vagina explode.

"Oh God, Cole," she cried his name, then heard his hard exclamation of pleasure, knew he was coming, knew her climax had triggered his own as well.

"Tess," he groaned. "Damn you, when I get hold of you I'll fuck you until you can't walk."

Tess trembled at the erotic promise in his voice, the dark sensuality that terrified her, made her want to give him whatever he wanted.

"No," she whispered, fighting for breath, fighting for sanity. "I asked you to stay away."

She wanted to whimper, she wanted to beg.

There was silence over the line.

"Stay away?" he asked her carefully. "I don't think so, baby. I've stayed away too long as it is. You're mine Tess, and I'm going to prove it to you. All mine. In every way mine, and I'll be damned if I'll let you deny it any longer."

# Chapter Three

** හ**

Her mother was waiting on her when she came down the stairs, her suitcase in hand. Ella Delacourte was a small, spare woman, with dark brown hair and sharp hazel eyes. There were few things she missed, and even less that she was tolerant of.

"So you're still going," she snapped out as she eyed the suitcase Tess set by the front door. "I thought you would have more pride than that, Tess."

Tess pressed her lips together as she fought to keep her sarcastic reply in check.

"This has nothing to do with pride, Mother," she told her quietly. "He's still my father."

"The same father who destroyed your family. Who ensured you lost the home you were raised in," Ella reminded her bitterly. "The same father that married the whore who meant more to him than you did."

Tess's chest clenched with pain, and with anger. She wasn't a child anymore, and there were times when she could clearly see why her father had been unable to get along with her mother. Ella saw only one view, and that was hers.

"He took care of us, Mother," she pointed out. "Even after the divorce."

"As though he had a choice." Ella crossed her arms over her breasts as she stared at Tess in anger.

"Yes, Mother, he had a choice after I reached eighteen," Tess reminded her bleakly. "But I believe he still sends you money and provides whatever you need, just as he does me. He doesn't have to do this."

"Conscience money," Ella spat out, her pretty face twisting into lines of anger and bitter fury. "He knows he did us wrong, Tess. He threw us out—"

"No, you elected to leave, if I remember correctly." Tess wanted to scream in frustration.

The argument never ended. It was never over. She felt as though she continually paid for her father's choices because her mother had no way of making him pay.

"He's depraved. As though you need to spend a week in his house." Ella was shaking now with fury, contempt lacing each word out of her mouth. "Those parties he throws are excuses for orgies, and that wife of his—"

"I don't want to hear it, Mother—"

"You think your father and his new family are so respectable and kind," she sneered. "You think I don't know how you watched that brother of hers. That I didn't know about the flowers he sent you last year. They're monsters, Tess." She pointed a thin, accusing finger at Tess. "Depraved and conscienceless. He'll turn you into a tramp."

Tess felt her face flame. She had fought for years to hide her attraction to Cole. She had heard all the rumors, knew his sexual exploits were often gossiped about. He had more or less admitted them to her on several occasions.

"No one can turn me into a tramp, Mother," she bit out. "Just as there's no way you can change the fact that I have a father. I can't ignore him or pretend he doesn't exist, and I don't want to."

Tess faced her parent, feeling the same, horrible fear that always filled her at the thought of making her too angry. Of disappointing her in any way. But as she faced her fear, she felt her own anger festering inside her. For so many years she had tried to make up for the divorce her father had somehow forced. She knew he took the blame for it. Just as her mother vowed complete innocence. She was beginning to wonder if either of them would ever tell her the truth.

"You'll end up just like him," Ella accused, her eyes narrowing hatefully.

Tess could only shake her head.

"I'll be home in a week, Mother," she said, picking up her luggage.

In the back of her mind, she knew she would not be returning though. She had stayed out of guilt and out of fear of failing somehow in her mother's eyes. She was only now realizing, she could never succeed in her mother's opinion though. She was fighting a losing battle. A battle she didn't want to win to begin with.

\* \* \* \* \*

Tess was still trembling when she pulled into the large circular driveway of her father's home. The shadows of evening were washing over his stately Virginia mansion, spilling long shadows over the three-story house and the tree shrouded yard. The drive from New York wasn't a hard one, but her nervousness left her feeling exhausted. She definitely wasn't up to facing Cole. Her face flushed at the thought. She had tried not to think about the phone call that morning, or the core of heat it had left lingering inside her.

It had nearly been enough to have her turning around several times and heading back to her safe, comfortable life in her mother's home. She would have too, until she thought of her mother. Ella was too frightened of the world to draw her head out of her books and see the things she was missing. She had lost her husband years before their divorce because of her distaste of his sexual demands. She told Tess often how disgusting, how shameful she found sex to be.

Tess didn't want to grow old, knowing she had passed up the exciting things in life. She didn't want to ache all her life for the one thing she needed the most and passed up. But she didn't want her heart broken. And Tess had a feeling Cole could break her heart.

She wanted him too badly. She had realized that in the past months. The dreams were driving her crazy. Dreams of Cole tying her to his bed, teasing her, touching her, his dark voice whispering his sexual promises to her. She was awaking more and more often, her cunt soaked, her breathing ragged, a plea on her lips.

Tess had known he was bad news even before her father married his sister. His eyes were too wicked, his looks too sensual. He was wickedly sexy, sinfully sensuous. She moaned in rising excitement and fear.

Leaving her keys in the ignition for the butler to park it, Tess jumped from the car. Night was already rolling in, and she would be damned if she would sit out in that car because she was too scared to walk into the house. Hopefully, Cole wouldn't be there. He wasn't always there.

"Good evening, Miss Delacourte." The butler, a large, burly ex-bouncer opened the door for her as she stepped up to it.

Thomas was well over fifty, Tess knew, but he didn't look a day over thirty-five. He was six feet tall, heavily muscled and sported a crooked nose and several small scars on his broad face. He was Irish, he said, with a mix of Cherokee Indian and German ancestry. His thick, brown hair was in a crew cut, his large face creased with a smile.

"Good evening, Thomas. Is Father in?" She stepped into the house, more uncomfortable than she had thought she would be.

This was the home she had grown up in, the one she had raced through with the puppy her father had once bought her, but her mother had gotten rid of. The home where her father had once patched skinned knees and a bruised heart. The home her mother had taken her out of when her father demanded his rights as a husband, or a divorce.

"Your father and Mrs. Delacourte are out for the evening, Miss," he told her as she stepped into the house. "Will you be staying for a while?"

"Yes." She took a deep breath. "My luggage is outside. Is my room still available?"

There was an edge of pain as she asked the question. She had learned that Missy had opened her room for guests, rather than keeping it up for Tess's infrequent returns.

"I'm sorry, Miss Tess," Thomas said softly. "The room is being redecorated. But the turret room is available. I prepared it myself this morning."

The turret room was the furthest away from the guest or family bedrooms. At the back of the house, on the third floor. The turret had been added decades ago by her grandfather and she had loved it as a child. Now she resented the fact that it was not a family room, but the one she knew Missy used for those visitors she could barely tolerate. Evidently, Tess thought, she had slipped a few notches in her stepmother's graces.

Tess breathed in deeply. Those weren't tears clogging her throat, she assured herself. Her chest was tight from exhaustion, not pain.

"Fine." She swallowed tightly. "Could you have my luggage brought up? I need a shower and some sleep. I'll see Father in the morning."

"Of course, Miss Tess." Thomas' voice was gentle. He had been with the family for as long as she could remember and she knew she wasn't hiding her pain from him.

"Is Father happy, Thomas?" she asked him as she paused before going down the hall to the hidden staircase that led to the turret room. "Does Missy take care of him?"

"Your father seems very happy to me, Miss Tess," Thomas assured her. "Happier than I've seen since Mrs. Ella left."

Tess nodded abruptly. That was all that mattered. She moved quickly down the hall, turning toward the kitchen then entering the staircase to the right. The staircase led to one place. The turret room.

It was a beautiful room. Rounded and spacious, the furniture had been made to fit the room exactly. The bed was large with a heavy, rounded walnut headboard that sat perfectly against the wall. Heavy matching drawers slid into the stone wall for a dresser, with a mantle above it to the side of the bed. Across the room was a small fireplace, the wood was gas logs, but it was pretty enough.

She felt like Cinderella before the Prince rescued her. Tess sat down heavily on the quilt that covered the bed. This sucked. She should get back in her car and head straight back home where she belonged. She didn't belong here anymore, and she was beginning to wonder if she ever had.

Taking a deep breath, she ran her hands through her hair and listened to Thomas coming up the stairs. He stepped into the room with a friendly smile, but his brown eyes were somber as they met hers.

"Will you be okay here, Miss Tess?" he asked her as he set the large suitcase and matching overnight bag on the luggage rack beside the door. "I could quickly freshen another room."

"No. I'm fine, Thomas." She shook her head. What was the point? She had come back, mainly to find something that didn't exist. It was best she learn that now, before it went any further.

Thomas nodded before going to the fireplace. With practiced moves he lit the gas fire, then pulled back and nodded in satisfaction at the even heat coming off the ceramic logs.

"Would you like me to announce dinner for you, Miss Tess?" he asked.

Her father and stepmother were away. Tess knew the servants would only be preparing their own food. She shook her head. They were all most likely anticipating a night to relax, she wouldn't deprive them of that. What hurt the most was her father's absence. He had known she was coming, and he wasn't here. It was the first time he had ever left, knowing she was coming home. The first time Tess had ever felt as though she were a stranger in her own home.

* * * * *

One thing Tess really liked about the turret room was the bathroom. The huge room was situated to the right of the bed, and held a large sunken tub big enough for three and a fully mirrored wall. Thomas had stocked the small refrigerator unit against her objections. One of his little surprises was a bottle of her favorite white wine. Tess opened it, poured a full glass and sipped at it as the water ran into the large ceramic tub. Steam rose around the room, creating an ethereal effect with the glow of the candles she had lit.

She stripped out of her jeans and T-shirt and setting the wineglass and bottle on a small shelf, sank into the bubbled liquid. Exquisite. She leaned back against the hand fashioned back of the tub and rested her head on the pillowed headrest. It was hedonistic. A wicked, sinful extravagance, as her mother would have said.

She closed her eyes and took a deep breath. She had expected her father to be home, had expected some sort of greeting. She didn't expect to be left on her own. But the sinful richness of the bathtub eased a bit of the hurt. She could enjoy this. This one last time.

She hadn't come home without ulterior motives, she knew. Perhaps this was her payment for it. It wasn't her father that had drawn her so much as the man that she knew would arrive sooner or later.

Cole. She took a deep breath, flushing once again at the memory of the phone conversation. She could handle a little sex with him. It wasn't like she was a virgin. It was the rest of it. Cole didn't go for just sex. Cole was wild and kinky and liked to spice things up, she had heard. Heard. She whimpered, remembering his promise to tie her to his bed and what he would do there.

She had never had rough sex, though she admitted, she had never had satisfying sex either. It had never been intense enough, strong enough. The hardest climax of her life had been in that damned hallway, with Cole's fingers thrusting inside her cunt. She had been so slick, so wet, that even her thighs had been coated with it.

Lifting the wineglass from the shelf, Tess sipped at it a bit greedily. Her skin was sensitive, her breasts swollen with arousal, her cunt clenching in need. Dammit, she should have found a nice, tame principal or teacher to satisfy her lusts with. Cole was bad news. She knew he was bad news. Had always known it.

She had known Cole before her father had married his sister. She had heard about his sexual practices, his pleasures. He was hedonistic, wicked. And sometimes, he liked to dominate. He wasn't a bully outside the bedroom. Confident, superior, but not a bully. But she had heard rumors. Tales of Cole's preferences, his insistence on submission from his women. The comments he had made to her over the years only backed up the rumors she had heard.

Tess trembled at the thought of being dominated by Cole. Equal parts fear and excitement thrummed through her veins, her cunt, swelling her breasts, making her nipples hard. She didn't need this. Didn't need the desire for him that she was feeling. Didn't need the broken heart she knew he could deal her. She drained the wine from her glass then poured another, realizing the effects of the drink were already beginning to travel through her system. She felt more relaxed, finally. She hadn't been this relaxed in months. Enjoying the sensations, she poured another, hoping she would at least manage a few hours of sleep tonight without dreaming of Cole.

# Chapter Four

**ℰᴖ**

Tess came downstairs the next morning expecting to be greeted by her father. She had dressed in the dove gray sweater dress he had sent her the month before. Tiny pearl buttons closed it from the hem to just above her breasts. On her feet she wore matching pumps and pearls at her neck. Confident and sure of herself, Tess felt able to field her father's questions, his urgings that she move back home for a while. When she walked into the dimly lit family room, it was Cole she found instead.

She stood still, silent as she faced him across the room. His eyes, a brilliant blue and filled with wicked secrets, watched her narrowly. Thick, black lashes framed the brilliant orbs, just as his thick, black hair framed the savage features of his face. His cheekbones were high, sharp, his nose an arrogant slash down his face. His lips were wide, and could be full and sensual or thin with anger. Now, he seemed merely curious.

His arms were crossed over his wide, muscular chest, his ankles crossed as he stood propped against the back of a sectional couch that faced away from her.

"Where's Father?" Tess asked him, fighting her excitement, her own unruly desires.

"He was held up. He expects, perhaps, to be home tomorrow," he told her quietly.

"Perhaps?" She barely stilled the tremble in her voice.

"Perhaps." He straightened from his lazy stance, watching her with a narrow-eyed intensity that had her breasts and her cunt throbbing. Damn him for the effect he had on her.

"So he couldn't tell me himself?" she questioned him nervously, watching him advance on her, determined to stand her ground.

"I'm sure he'll call, eventually." His voice was a slow, lazy drawl, thick with tension and arousal. It was all she could do to keep her eyes on his face, rather than allowing them to lower to see how thick the bulge in his pants had grown. She knew for certain the throb in her vagina had intensified.

"So you volunteered as the welcome wagon?" She was breathless, and knew he could hear it in her voice. His eyes darkened with the knowledge, causing her heartbeat to intensify.

He moved steadily nearer, until he was only inches from her. She could feel the warmth of his body, and it tingled over her nerve endings. He was tall, so much broader than she. She felt at once threatened and secure. The alternating emotions had her caught, unable to move, unwilling to run.

The blood raced through her veins as she attempted to make sense of the powerful feelings racing through her body and her mind. Two years she had thought about him, fought the temptation he represented and the heat he inspired.

"I'm always here to welcome you, Tess." He smiled, that slow quirk of his lips that made the muscles in her stomach tighten. "But I have to admit, I was more than eager after talking to you yesterday."

Her face flamed. Echoes of her whimpers, her fight to breathe through her climax whispered through her mind. Cole's voice, husky and deep, urging her on, rough from his own arousal, then his own climax.

Tess swallowed hard as she caught her lip between her teeth in nervous indecision. Did she reach out for him? Should she run from him?

"Hound dog," she muttered, more angry at herself than she was at him.

He chuckled, his hand reaching out to touch the bare flesh at her neck.

"Prickly as ever I see," he said with a vein of amusement as his eyes darkened. "Would you be as hot in bed, Tess?"

"Like I would tell you!" she bit out.

She fought the instinct to lean closer to him, to inhale the spicy scent of aroused, determined male.

"Hmm, maybe you would show me," he suggested, his voice silky smooth, heated.

Tess trembled at the low, seductive quality of his voice. It traveled through her body, tightening her cunt, making her breasts swell, the nipples bead in anticipation. Her entire body felt flushed, hot. Then the breath became trapped in her throat. His hand moved, the backs of his fingers caressing a trail of fire to the upper mounds of her heaving breasts.

He looked into her eyes, his own slumberous now, heavy lidded.

"Mine," he whispered.

Her eyes widened at the possessive note in his voice.

"I don't think so." She wanted to wince at the raspy, rough quality of her voice. "I belong to no man, Cole. Least of all you."

So why was her body screaming out in denial? She could feel the bare lips of her cunt moistening as her body prepared itself for his possession. Her skin tingled, her mouth watered at the thought of his kiss.

"All mine," he growled as a single button slid free of its fragile mooring over her heaving breasts. "You knew there was no way I would stay away after hearing you climax to the sound of my voice, Tess. You knew I wouldn't let you go."

She shrugged, fighting for her composure, an independence that seemed more ingrained than needed at the moment.

"You don't have a choice but to let me go," she informed him, feeling trepidation dart through her at the sudden intensity in his eyes.

His fingers stroked over the rounded curve of her breast, his expression thoughtful as he stared down at her.

"Why are you fighting me, Tess?" he suddenly asked her softly. "For two years I've done everything but tie you down and make you admit to wanting me. And I know you do. So why are you fighting it?"

"Maybe I want to be tied down and forced to admit it," she said flippantly, ignoring the flare of excitement in her vagina at the thought. She had heard the rumors, knew the accusations her mother had heaped on her father's brother-in-law for years. "Yeah, Cole, me tied down, just waiting for you and one of your best buds. Hey hon, the possibilities are limitless here."

Her mouth was the bane of her existence. She mentally rolled her eyes at the sharp, mocking declaration.

"My best bud, huh?" He tilted his head, watching her with a slight smile.

"The more the merrier." She moved away from him, denying herself the touch she wanted above all others. "You know how it is. A girl has to have some kind of excitement in her life. May as well go all the way."

She was going to cut her own tongue out. Tess felt more possessed than in possession of any common sense at the moment. Tempting Cole, pushing him, was never a good idea. She knew that from experience. Yet it seemed she knew how to do little else.

"Tess, be careful what you wish for." He was openly laughing at her. "Have you ever had two men at once, baby?"

The endearment, softly spoken in that dark, wicked voice sent her pulse racing harder than before.

"Does it matter?" She turned back to him, some demonic imp urging her to tease, to tempt in return.

She flashed him a look from beneath her lashes, touching at his hips, suppressing her groan at the size of the erection beneath his jeans. Damn, he was going to bust the zipper any minute now.

"Doesn't matter." He crossed his arms over his chest. "I can give you whatever you want, Sugar. If you really want it. I'm flexible."

* * * * *

Cole felt his dick throb. Damn her, he knew she had no idea how far she truly was pushing him. He could see the excitement in her eyes, a glimmer of sexual heat, of determination. Did she think she could turn him off by giving him carte blanche to do his worse? She had no idea how sexual he could get. The thought of tying her down, forcing her to admit the needs of her body, or his needs, was nearly more than his self-control could bear. The thought of introducing her to the pleasures of a *ménage a trois*, hearing her screams of pleasure echo in his ears, had his cock so hard it was a physical ache.

He wanted Tess to have every touch, every sexual experience she could ever imagine wanting to try. He wanted her hot, wet, and begging for his cock. He wanted her to admit to her needs, just as he finally admitted to his own. He wanted Tess, now, tomorrow, forever. However he could get her, every way she would let him have her.

Cole watched the flush that mounted her cheekbones, the flare of interest in her eyes that she quickly doused. She thought it a game, a sexual repartee that she could easily brush aside later. But it didn't change the fact that Tess had given such ideas more than a passing thought. He could see it in the hard rise and fall of her breasts, the swollen curve of them, the hard points of her nipples. They were nearly as hard as his cock.

She couldn't know, he thought with a thread of amusement, just how much he would enjoy doing both things with her. The dominance level he possessed was incredibly high. Introducing her to being tied down, teased, tormented, or sandwiching her between his body and Jesse's—

He had to forcibly tamp down his lust. Not that sharing her would be easy, or would happen often, but there was a particular pleasure in it that could be found in no other sexual act. The thought of total control of her body, her desires and her lusts was an aphrodisiac nearly impossible to resist.

"Tess, you shouldn't dare me," he warned her carefully. "You don't know what you could be asking for, baby."

He felt honor bound to give her one chance, and one chance only, to still the raging desires building inside him. She didn't know, couldn't know the sexuality that was so much a part of him. A sexuality and dark desire he had been willing to dampen for her. But her bold declaration that she could handle them was more than he could resist.

"Maybe I do know." He loved the breathless quality in her voice, the edge of fear and lust in her voice was a heady combination.

"I would fuck your ass, Tess," he growled advancing on her once again. "Is that what you want? My best bud sinking in that tight pussy while I push inside your back hole. You would scream, baby."

The idea of it was making him so hot he could barely stand the heat himself.

"Hmm..." Her pink lips pouted into a moue of thoughtfulness. "Sounds interesting, Cole. But you know, I couldn't allow just anyone such privileges." She sighed regretfully. "Sorry, darling, but it appears you're out of luck."

Oh, she was in trouble. Cole kept his expression only slightly amused, allowing his sweet Tess to dig her own grave.

"And what qualities must a man have to be so lucky?" he asked her as he deliberately maneuvered her against the wall, his body pressing against hers, not forcing her, but holding her, warming her.

For a moment, an endearing vulnerability flashed in her eyes. His heart softened at what he read there. Mingled hope and need, a flash of uncertainty.

"Something you don't have." He wondered if she heard the regret in her voice.

"And what would that be, baby?" He wanted to pull her to his chest, hold her, assure her that anything she needed, anything she wanted, was hers for the asking.

She pushed away from him, her natural defensiveness taking over again, that flash of pain in her eyes overriding her need to play, to tease and tempt.

"Heart, Cole. It takes a heart," she bit out. "And I really don't think you have one."

* * * * *

Tess walked away quickly, anger enveloping her. It did little to tamp the desire or the raging cauldron of emotions that threatened to swamp her. Damn. Double damn. She couldn't love him. She couldn't need his love. Two years of sparring with him, fighting his advances and his heated looks couldn't have caused this.

She felt her body trembling, her chest tightening with tears. Loving Cole was hopeless. She didn't stand a chance against the sophisticated, experienced women he often slept with. She had seen them, hated them. Knowing he took them to his bed, made them scream for his touch was more than she could bear. Surely she didn't love him. But Tess had a very bad feeling she did.

# Chapter Five

ॐ

Tess came awake hours later, a sense of being watched, studied, breaking through the erotic dream of Cole teasing her, tempting her with a kiss that never came. On the verge of screaming out for it, the presence in her room began to make itself felt.

She blinked her eyes open, frowning at the soft light of a candle on the small half moon table by her bed. Her head turned, her heart began to race. Cole was sitting on the side of the bed watching her, his blue eyes narrowed, his muscular chest bare except for the light covering of black hair that angled down his stomach and disappeared into— Her eyes widened, then flew back to his. He was naked. Sweet God, he was naked and sporting a hard on that terrified her. Thick and long, the head purpled, the flesh heavily veined.

Tess was suddenly more than aware of her nakedness beneath the heavy quilt. When she had gone to bed, she had thought nothing of it. Now she could feel her breasts swelling, her nipples hardening. Between her legs, she felt the slow, heated moistening of her fevered flesh. She felt something else, too. Her arms were tied to the curved headboard, stretched out, the same as her legs, with very little play in the rope. Son of a bitch, he had tied her on her bed like some damned virginal sacrifice.

"What have you done?" She cleared the drowsiness from her voice as he sat still, watching her with those wicked, sensually charged eyes. "Untie me, Cole. What are you doing here?"

"First lesson," he told her, his voice soft as his lips quirked in a sexy grin. "Are you ready for it?"

"Lesson?" She shook her head, her voice filled with her surging anger. How dare the son of a bitch tie her up? "What the hell are you talking about, Cole?"

His hand lifted. Tess thought he would touch her, grab her, instead, those long fingers wrapped around his cock absently, stroking it. She swallowed tightly, her mouth watering, aching to feel that bulging head in it. She may have even considered giving into the impulse, if she could have moved her body.

"Your first lesson in being my woman, Tess," he told her, his voice cool, determined. "I told you I was tired of waiting on you. Tonight, your first lesson begins."

Tess rolled her eyes as she breathed out in irritation.

"Are you a secret psycho or something, Cole?" she bit out. "Did you just pay attention to what you said? Now let me go and stop acting so weird. Dammit, if you wanted to fuck, you should have just said so."

He smiled at her. The bastard just smiled that slow, wicked grin of his.

"But, Tess, I don't want to just fuck," he said, his voice amused. "I want you know who controls your body, your lusts. I want you to know, all the way to your soul, who owns that pretty pussy, that tempting little ass and hot mouth. I want you to admit they're mine, and mine alone to fuck however I please."

Damn. She knew Cole was into kink, but rape?

"Cole." She fought to keep her voice reasonable. "This is no way to go about getting a woman, hon. Really. You know, flowers, courtship, that's the way to a woman's heart."

"Really?" He was openly laughing at her now. "I sent you flowers, darling—"

Her eyes widened.

"Oh yeah, with a card telling me what size butt plug to buy so you could fuck my ass," she bit out as she jerked at the ropes binding her ankles. "Real romantic, Cole."

s stilled, quivering, seeing the lust, the excitement
ole's face. His cock was huge, thick and long, and she
would stretch her pussy until she was screaming for
ut her ass? No way. From the look on Cole's face
he had figured out the way of it, exactly.

She remembered her sense of horror, the shameful
excitement when she read the card. She had dumped flowers
and all in the trash, but kept the card. Why, she wasn't certain.

He shrugged easily. "Practical," he told her. "I wanted
you prepared. But since you were unwilling to prepare
yourself, then you'll just have to accept the pain."

Pain? No. No pain.

"Now look, Cole," she warned him reasonably. "Father
will be really pissed with you. And you know I'll tell—"

"I asked your father's permission first, Tess," he told her
softly, his expression patient now. "Why do you think your
mother finally left your father? She refused to accept who he
was and what he needed. I will not make that mistake with
you. You will know, and you will accept to your soul, your
needs as well as my own. You won't run from me. Your father
understands this, and he's giving me the time I need to help
you understand."

Tess stared up at Cole, fury welling inside her as her arms
jerked at the ropes that held her. Damn him, they weren't
tight, but there wasn't a chance she could smack that damned
superior expression off his face.

"You're lying to me," she accused him. "Father would
never let you hurt me."

"Ask him in the morning." He shrugged lazily. "You'll be
free by then."

A sense of impotency filled her. Damn him, he thought he
had all the damned answers and all the damned plans. She
wasn't a toy for him to play with, and she would show him
that.

"I'll have you arrested," she promised him. "I swear, if it's
the last thing I do I'll have you locked up."

He was quiet for long moments, his eyes glittering with
lust, with cool knowledge.

"I wouldn't do that if I were you. And I think come
morning, perhaps you will have changed your mind."

Tess breathed in hard, watching him with a sense of fear, and hating the arousal that it brought her.

"What are you talking about?" she bit out.

His hand ceased the lazy stroking of his cock, then moved to her stomach. Her muscles clenched involuntarily at the heat and calloused roughness of his flesh.

"Tonight, I'll give you a taste of what's coming," he promised her. "You'll learn, Tess, who your master is, slowly. A step at a time. Nothing too hard, baby, I promise."

Tess shivered. He didn't sound cruel, but he was determined. His voice was soft, immeasurably gentle, but filled with purpose. He would have her now, and he would have her on his terms.

"This isn't what I want, Cole," she said, fighting for breath, for a sense of control.

His hand moved lazily from her stomach, his eyes tracking each move, his fingers trailing between her thighs until one ran through the thick, slick cream that proved her words false. She trembled, biting back a moan of pleasure as the thick length of his finger dipped into her vagina.

"Isn't it?" he whispered. "I think you're lying, Tess. You shouldn't lie to me, baby."

Before Tess knew what was coming, his hand moved, then the flat of his palm delivered a stinging blow to the bare flesh of her cunt.

Tess jerked at the heat. "You son of a bitch," she screamed, jerking against her bond, ignoring the lash of pleasure that made her clit swell further. "I'll kick your ass when I get out of here."

Cole grinned, then moved from her side to position himself between her spread thighs.

"Let me go, you bastard!" she bit out, fighting to ignore the shameful pleasure and anticipation rising inside her.

"Naughty Tess," he whispered, her cunt, sliding over the moisture th her pussy lips. "You're tight, Tess. F you had a lover?"

"Kiss my ass!" she cried out, the palm landed on the upper curve of ropes, terrified of the shocking vibra that radiated from the heat of the blo

Her body arched as his finger s again. It was a slow stroke, the l muscles, making the flesh tremble fought the need to whimper, to beg a

"How long, Tess, since you've l again.

Tess realized she was pantin climax. God, if he would just let her

"I hate you," she growled.

His finger stopped. Halfway clenching desperately in need, and h

"You aren't being nice, Tess," leave you tied here, hot and hurting you what you need, eventually. N How long?"

The threat was clear. His finge watched her, his expression har retained that lazy, gentle humor. frightening.

"Four years. Satisfied—Oh Go head digging into the pillows as hi smooth, forceful plunge.

Tess was shuddering, her clima pulsing in desperation.

"Damn you're tight, Tess." His the sensitive depths as she writhe tight as a virgin. I bet your ass is eve

# Chapter Six

"Cole, let's be reasonable," Tess panted, her cunt clenching over the finger lodged inside it, quivering from the deep, gentle strokes his fingertip was administering. "Your cock will not fit there. Stop trying to scare me."

But she had a feeling it wasn't an idle threat.

He smiled. She knew better than to trust that smile. It was a slow curve of his lips, a crinkle at the corners of his eyes. Watching her carefully, he slid his finger from the soaked depths of her hot channel and then moved to lie down beside her.

Tess watched him carefully, like a wild beast as he propped his head on his arm and watched her through narrowed eyes. Then his gaze shifted, angling to her thighs, her eyes following as his hand moved.

"No—" she cried out helplessly as his hand raised.

She jerked. His head moved, his lips latching on a hard, pointed nipple a second before he delivered another stinging blow to the wet lips of her cunt.

She cried out, pleasure and pain dragging a helpless sound of confused desire from her lips as her body bowed and she jerked against him. His tongue rasped her nipple as he suckled her, and the next blow to her cunt was delivered to the flesh that shielded her swollen clit. Her cry was louder, her body jerking, arching, fighting both pain and pleasure as she struggled to separate the two. She was on fire, her head reeling from the confusing morass of sensations. She wanted to beg for more, beg for mercy.

Another blow struck her, his palm angled to deliver the blow from her clit to her vagina as he pinched her nipple

Lora Leigh

between his teeth. The stinging pain, hot and fierce had her clit throbbing as she screamed from a near climax.

"Please," she begged, her head thrashing against the pillow as she felt his arm rise again. "Please, Cole—"

A strangled scream left her throat as the hardest blow landed, striking with force and fire, sending her clit blazing, her orgasm peaking against her will. It shuddered through her body as his palm ground into her clit with just enough pressure to trigger her release.

Then his lips covered hers with a groan, his tongue spearing into her mouth with greed and hunger. Tess fought to get closer, her arms and legs protesting their confinement as she met his kiss with equal voraciousness, her tongue tangling with his, her moans a harsh rasp against her throat as she felt her cunt throb, her vagina ache for more.

Tess shuddered with the throbbing intensity of her climax, a distant part of her was shocked, amazed that she could respond in such a way. Fiery tingles of sensation coursed over her body, licked at her womb, left her greedy, hungry for more. Her cunt was empty, a gnawing ache of arousal tormenting it now. It wasn't enough. She needed more. So much more.

"Do you need more, Tess??" he growled as he pulled back and stared down at her.

His eyes were no longer patient, they were hot and hungry, watching her intently.

"More. Please, Cole. I need you," she moaned staring up at him as her body moved restlessly, needing him, wanting his cock until she could barely breathe, her arousal was so intense.

He moved back, his hand going between her thighs, a ravenous groan coming from his throat as he felt the thick layer of cream that now coated her flesh.

"Your pussy's so hot, Tess." His voice sounded tortured. "So hot and sweet, I could make a meal of you now."

"Yes." She twisted against him, needing him to touch her, to fuck her, to relieve the yawning pit of exquisite need throbbing inside her.

"Not yet," he denied her, making her whimper. "Not yet, baby. But soon. Real soon."

She watched as he moved from her, going to his knees then propping her pillows beneath her shoulders and head.

"You know what I want, Tess," he told her, his voice rough, his cock aiming for her lips. "Open your mouth, baby, give me what I want."

Anything. Anything to convince him to relieve the ache that throbbed clear to her stomach. Her lips opened, and she moaned as the thick head pushed past them, stretching them wider. He was huge, so long and thick she wanted to cry out in fear, scream at him to hurry and fuck her with it.

"Oh yeah, such a hot little mouth," he groaned, wrapping his fingers around the base as he penetrated her mouth, stopping only when her eyes began to widen with the fear he would choke her. "Relax your throat, Tess," he urged her. "Just one more inch, baby. Take one more inch for me and I'll show you how good I can make you feel next."

Her pussy throbbed out her answer. *Yes, take more, bitch. Take it all so he'll fuck me.* The ravenous creature that was her cunt demanded her obedience as fiercely as Cole did. Breathing through her nose, her eyes on his, she slowly relaxed the muscles of her throat, feeling him by slow increments give her the final inch he demanded she take.

His hand tightened on his cock, his finger brushing her mouth as he marked her limit, and still there was so much more. He pulled back as Tess suckled the thick length, her tongue washing over it, rasping the underside of his dick as he nearly pulled free of her mouth until she was slurping on nothing but the engorged head, and loving it.

Then he began to penetrate again. A slow measured thrust that sank his cock to the depth he marked, his expression tightening with such extreme pleasure that she fought to caress the broad head that attempted to choke her. She let her throat make a swallowing motion, a tentative movement to test her ability to do it.

Cole groaned, his dick jerking in her mouth as he pulled back, thrust home again. She repeated the movement, watching his face, never letting go of his expression as he began to fuck her mouth. He was panting, his teeth clenched, his hard stomach clenching.

"Yes, swallow it," he growled when she repeated the motion. "Swallow it, baby. Show me you want my cock."

He was fucking her mouth harder now, her lips stretched so wide they felt bruised, but Tess loved the feeling, loved watching the excitement, the extreme lust that crossed his face each time her throat caressed the head of his cock. His hips were bucking against her, his voice a rumbled growl as he fucked her lips, pushing his cock as deep as it could go, groaning as the flesh tensed, tightened further.

"Yes. I'm going to cum now, Tess. I'm going to cum in your hot little mouth just like I'm going to cum up that tight little ass. Take it, baby, take my cock." He speared in, she swallowed, his hips jerked, then Tess felt the first hard, hot blast of his semen rocket against the back of her throat. It was followed by more. Thick hard pulses of creamy cum spurted down her throat as he cried out above her.

Tess was ecstatic, quivering with anticipation as she felt his cock, still hard, pull out of her mouth. He would fuck her now. Surely, he would fuck her now.

"You're so beautiful, Tess," he whispered as he moved away from her, staring down at her, his eyes gentle once again. "So damned hot and beautiful, you make me crazy."

"Good," she moaned. "Fuck me now, Cole. Please."

He smiled, and her eyes widened as he shook his head.

"What?" she bit out, incredulously. "Damn you, Cole, you can't leave me like this."

"Did I say I was leaving you?" he asked her, arching his brow in question. "No, Tess, I'll be here with you, all night, every night. But you're not ready to be fucked yet."

"I promise I am," she bit out. "I really am, Cole." If she got any more ready, she would go up in flames.

He chuckled, though the sound was strained.

"Not yet, Tess," he whispered. "But soon."

He moved across the room, and then Tess noticed the small tray that sat on the mantle of her wall-enclosed dresser. He picked it up and as he turned back to her, Tess's eyes widened in apprehension.

There were several sexual aids laying on the silver tray, as well as a large tube of lubrication. The one that frightened her most, was the thick butt plug that sat on its wide base. Tess trembled at the sight of it, shaking her head in fear as he neared her. If only she was frightened enough, she thought distantly. God help her, her cunt was on fire, her body so sensitive she thought a soft breeze would send her into climax. And seeing those toys, the thick butt plug and the large dildo, had her trembling, not just in fear, but in excitement.

He set the tray on her nightstand, then sat on her bed, staring at it.

"If you don't stay aroused, needing me and what I'll give you, then I'll walk away," he said, his voice so soft she had to strain to hear it. "But I'll push you, Tess, see what you like, see what you can take. Not just tonight, but all week. You're mine until the night of your father's party. No matter what, no matter when, as long as what I'm doing arouses you."

"And if it doesn't?" she asked angrily. "What are you going to do, hurt me until I can't take it anymore?"

He turned to her, his eyes blazing.

"Only I can give you what you want, what you need," he bit out. "You're so damned hot to be dominated you can't stand it. Do you think I don't know that? Did you think you were told the rumors of my preferences needlessly? If you weren't excited by it, Tess, you wouldn't have been so wet you soaked my hand two years ago when I caught you in the hall. You're just scared of it. And I want you too damned bad to let you stay frightened of what we both need any longer."

"I won't do it!" But excitement was electrifying her body, making every cell throb in anticipation.

"Won't you?" he growled. "I know about the books your mother found in your room when you went to college, Tess. The stories you read, to satisfy that craving you couldn't explain."

Her face flushed. Her mother had been enraged over the naughty books she had found in Tess's room that year.

"Captives, dominated by their lovers. Submissive, loving every stroke of the sensual pleasure they received.

Tess could feel her flush of mortification staining her entire body.

"Did you ever fuck your ass, Tess?" he asked her softly, leaning toward her, watching her closely. "As you stroked your cunt, fighting for orgasm, did your finger ever steal into that hot, dark little passage, just to see what it felt like?"

She had. Tess moaned in humiliation. But it hadn't been her finger, rather it had been the rounded, slender vibrator she kept hidden. The dark surge of pleasure that had spread through her had been terrifying. Even worse had been the hard, shocking quake of an orgasm that had her nearly screaming, ripping through her body, and making her cunt gush its slick, sticky fluid. The remembered pain of the penetration, the humiliation of that rushing liquid squirting from her had caused her to never try such a thing again except with her fingers. Even now, years later, the thought of that one act was enough to leave her flushing with shame.

"Did it hurt, Tess?" And of course, those wicked eyes knew the flush of admission on her skin. "Did it make you want more?"

"No," she bit out, shaking with nerves, with arousal.

"I think it did." He touched her cheek, his fingers caressing her flesh, his voice gentle. "I think I left you aching, needing, and too damned scared to try to reach for it. I think, Tess, that you need me just as much as I need you."

"And I think you're crazy," she bit out, refusing him, wondering why she was when she needed it so damned bad.

His thumb stroked over her swollen lips, his eyes dark, glittering in the light of the candle.

"Am I?" he asked her softly. "Let's see, Tess, just how crazy I am."

# Chapter Seven

ഔ

Tess watched Cole, trying to still the hard, rough breaths that shook her body. She couldn't seem to get enough oxygen, couldn't seem to settle the hard shudder of her pounding heart.

"There's a fine line that divides pleasure and pain," he told her as he removed the butt plug from the tray, and the tube of lubricant. "It's so slim, that if went about the right way, the pain adds to the pleasure, in a dark erotic manner."

He moved to the bottom of the bed. He loosened the ropes attached to the footboard, then grabbed her legs quickly before she could kick out at him. Ignoring her struggles and heated curses, within minutes he had her entire body flipped over, the ropes once again holding her in position as he tucked several pillows beneath her hips.

"You bastard." Her voice was strangled as crazed excitement shot through her body.

Her buttocks were arched to him now. She was spread, open to him, and the flares of fear and excitement traveling through her body had her terrified.

"God, Tess, you're beautiful," he growled from behind her, his voice rough, filled with lust. "Your little ass so pink and pretty. And I like how you keep your pussy waxed so soft and smooth. But I would have preferred to do it myself. >From now on, I'll take care of it for you."

Tess trembled, crying out. She should hate this. She should be screaming, begging him to stop, instead her body pulsed in need and desire, in anticipation.

"You shouldn't have waited so long to come back, Tess," he whispered as he kissed one full cheek of her ass. "You

170

shouldn't have made me wait so long, baby, because I won't be able to be as gentle as I would have been."

Her cunt pulsed at his words.

"And I'll have to punish you." She whimpered at the rising excitement in his voice. "But I would have anyway, Tess. Because I need to see that pretty ass all red and hot from my hand."

"No—" Despite her instinctive cry, his hand fell to the rounded cheek of her ass.

Heat flared across her flesh, then she screamed as his finger sank into her pussy a second later. She twisted, writhed against her bonds.

"You're so wet," he groaned. "So tight and hot, Tess. But by the time my cock sinks into your pretty pussy, you'll be tighter."

His hand struck again as the broad finger retreated from her quaking vagina. As the heat built in the flesh of her buttocks, his finger sank in again. Tess was crying out in fear and a wash of dark, erotic excitement. The blows weren't cruel, rather sharp and stinging, building a steady heat in her flesh.

"So pretty." He whacked the other side, then his finger thrust into her again.

She was so wet she was dripping. He alternated mild and stinging blows that kept her flinching in anticipation. Kept her flesh heated, the pain flaring through her body. A pain she hated, hated because the pleasure from it was driving her crazy. She could feel her juices rolling from her cunt, hear her cries echoing with needs she didn't want to name.

By the time he finished, her ass felt on fire, her hips were rolling, her cunt throbbing. She was dying of need. If he didn't fuck her soon, she would go crazy. She was burning, inside and out, a wave of fiery lust tormenting her loins as she fought the depraved pleasures of the spanking.

"Your ass is so pretty and red now," he groaned. "Damn, Tess, I like you like this, baby, all tied up for me, reddening, your cunt hot and tight and so wet it soaks my fingers." Two fingers plunged inside her.

"Cole—" Her cry was hoarse and desperate as her orgasm teetered her on an edge of agonized excitement.

"I'm going to put this butt plug up your ass now, Tess," he warned her as he drew his fingers from her body. "Then I'll fuck you, baby. I'll fuck you so deep and hard you won't ever leave me again."

Tess's head ground into her pillow as his hand separated her buttocks. She flinched at the feel of cold lubricant, then cried out again as his finger sank fully into the tight hole. It pinched, sent a flare of heat through her muscles that had her bucking into the thrust.

"Oh, Tess, your ass is so tight." He twisted his finger inside her, spreading the lubrication, stretching the muscles as she whimpered in distress. "It doesn't want to stretch, Tess. Such a pretty virgin hole."

As full as his finger filled her, how would she ever take more? She tightened on him in fear, then moaned as the heated pain made her cunt throb hotter. She was depraved. She should be terrified, fighting him, instead her whimpers were begging for more.

He repeated the lubrication several times as Tess fought to breathe past the pleasure and pain. She was ready to scream, to beg for more. She wanted to whisper the forbidden words. She bit her lip, panted, cried out as his finger finally withdrew.

"Tess, I want you to take a deep breath," he finally instructed her heatedly. "Relax when the plug starts in, it will ease the pain if it's too much for you at first."

"You're torturing me," she cried out, bucking against her ropes. She didn't want this now. She was too scared. The dark lust rolling over her was too intense, too frightening. "Stop, Cole. Let me go!"

"It's okay, Tess." His hand smoothed over her bottom then his fingers clenched, separating her again. "It's okay, baby. It's normal to be scared. Just relax."

"Cole—" She didn't know if her cry was in protest or in need as she felt the tapered head of the thick plug nestle against her tiny hole.

"It's going to hurt, Tess." His voice was dark, excited. "You're going to scream for me, and you're going to love it. I know you will, baby."

"Oh God." She tossed her head on the pillow but couldn't help allowing her body to relax marginally.

She felt the device begin to penetrate the tight hole. At first, the piercing sensation was mild, but as the length and thickness increased, the steady, building fire began to shoot through her body.

She tensed, but Cole didn't ease up. She cried out as it grew brighter, then began begging as pain bloomed in her anus. But she wasn't begging him to stop.

"It hurts," she screamed out. "Oh God, Cole. Cole please—"

He didn't relent, instead, the fingers of his other hand moved to her pulsing cunt. There, they stroked and petted her clit until she was thrusting, pushing into his hand, crying out as the movement pushed the plug deeper into her ass.

She could feel her muscles stretching, protesting but eventually giving way to the thick intruder invading it. She bucked against her ropes, rearing back, writhing under the lash of burning pain, and equally burning pleasure.

"Damn you!" Her voice was hoarse, enraged from the building kaleidoscope of sensations rushing through her body.

The fiery heat of the invasion, the slow steady buildup of pain, the resulting agonizing pleasure so overwhelmed her senses that she felt dazed with it, awash in a darkly sensual reality where nothing existed except the slow, steady invasion of her ass, and the soft, too light caresses to her throbbing clit.

Long minutes later she jerked harshly as the last inch of the plug passed the tight anal ring, leaving seven inches of hard thick dildo lodged inside her. She squirmed, fighting to accustom herself to the sensation. Cole chose that moment to land his hand heavily on her ass again. Tess screamed, her muscles tightening around the plug, inflicting a disastrous form of ecstasy.

"Now, Tess," Cole growled. "Now, I get to eat that pretty pussy."

# Chapter Eight

## ဢ

Tess's cries were echoing in his head, throbbing in his cock. Cole couldn't remember a time he had been so turned on, so hot and ready to fuck. He wanted to plunge his cock as deep, as hard up her tight cunt as he could. He wanted to slam it inside her, master her with the brutality of a fucking so lustful that she would find it impossible to leave the only man who could give it to her.

But he knew, the longer he could keep her hanging on the edge of the sensations ripping through her, the more she would crave it later. He was a slave to the need to be the one who pleasured her.

The piercing of her ass with that plug had been the most erotic, satisfying thing he had done in his life. He wondered if she was even aware of how loud she had begged for more. How many times she had pleaded with him to push it hard inside her, to take her. He doubted it. Submissives rarely remembered that first time, those first long minutes that the plug, or a hot, thick cock invaded their ass.

It was the pain and pleasure combined. The needs, so shocking, so consuming that they dazed the mind to the point that the submissive rarely remembered begging for it.

"Fuck me," Tess still begged, her voice was thick and desperate as her cunt leaked the honeyed cream of her need. And he would fuck her. Soon.

He lifted a small, oblong metal device from the tray. It was attached to a long cord with a control box at the end. A silver bullet it was called. So tiny it appeared harmless, but the effects of its internal vibrations would send Tess into such a haze of rapture that she would never forget it.

175

He inserted the three-inch long device into her cunt. His cock clenched at the closed fist tightness he encountered as he pressed it past the fullness of the plug lodged in her ass and moved it to the back of her cunt. He positioned the little device for maximum vibration against her G-spot then withdrew. He set the control on low, a gentle, stroking vibration that nonetheless caused her to flinch. Then he set about feeding himself from her cunt.

He lapped at her pussy, just as he had once promised her he would. Gentle strokes into her vagina with his tongue that had her bucking against his mouth, begging for more. Her body was sheened with sweat, her breathing harsh, her cries desperate as he tongued her, stroked her. And she tasted so damned good he couldn't help himself but to thrust his tongue as deep inside her as he could go, and draw more of her into his mouth.

Cole was on fire for her. He knew his control was slipping, something that never happened, something he had never had to fight to keep before. But he had to prepare her, he couldn't allow himself to unwittingly hurt her. Tess was everything to him. His heart, his soul, the happiness he had always believed he would never find. She teetered between erotic pain and the pain that could irrevocably damage her sexuality forever. If he wasn't careful, extremely careful, then he would destroy both of them. Because Cole knew he couldn't go much longer without her.

So he tamped down his own lusts, stroked her gently, gauged her need and advanced the speed of the vibrator accordingly. She was bucking in his hands now, nearing that point of no return. Reluctantly, he moved back from her dripping vagina, licked back, circled her clit with his tongue. Then he turned, laying on his back, positioning himself to suck the swollen, engorged bud into his mouth as he edged the speed of the vibrator higher.

She exploded, her body tensed. Her scream was strangled, breathless as her body bowed, jerked, then began a repeated shudder that signaled the beginning of her orgasm. He tightened his lips on her clit, flicked it with his tongue and held her hips with easy strength when the hot, volcanic rush of her release began to rush through her body.

* * * * *

Tess was dying. She knew she was dying and she eagerly embraced the exquisite rush of painful pleasure that threw her over the brink. Her body was jerking uncontrollably, her orgasm filling her body, pumping through her blood, spasming her uterus as it tore through her. She could feel the hard vibration inside her, Cole's lips at her clit, blending into a raging storm she knew she wouldn't survive. Hard shudders rushed over her, pleasure, unlike anything she could have conceived tore her apart. And in a distant part of her mind, she wondered if she would ever be the same again. If she survived it.

She screamed against the torrent, but couldn't fight it. She could feel her fluids gushing through her pussy as it spasmed, and Cole's mouth moving to catch them with a hard, male groan. His tongue speared inside her tortured cunt, triggering another hard shudder, another gush of fluids until finally, she collapsed mindlessly against her ropes, dazed, stripped of strength.

Small tremors still assaulted her boneless body. The never-ending pulse of her climax didn't go away easily. She could hear Cole, a hard, brutal male groan echoing through the room as his body jerked against her. Had he come? Had he been inside her and she didn't know it? It didn't matter. She was drifting on a haze of pleasure so weak, so astounding that she couldn't think, and didn't want to.

"Tess?" Cole's voice was tender, warm as he moved behind her. "Are you okay, baby?"

She felt the ropes loosening, his hands calloused and gentle on her skin as he untied her, helped her to stretch out on the bed. She lay boneless, so satiated she could barely move.

She was aware of Cole moving along the bed beside her, turning her over to her back, his expression, when she looked up at him, was concerned, gentle.

"Sleepy," she whispered. And she was. So tired, so emotionally and physically drained she could barely stay awake.

"Sleep, Tess." He kissed her cheek gently. "Rest, baby. We start again tomorrow."

\* \* \* \* \*

Cole lay down beside her, drawing the quilt over them, ignoring the pulse of his still throbbing cock. He had climaxed with Tess, but it wasn't enough. He needed to be buried inside her, feeling her, tight and hot, enclosing him with her satin heat.

And he knew the fight wasn't finished. Accepting the pain-filled pleasure would be the easy part for Tess. Submitting to him would be the hard part. Giving in to him, no matter what he asked of her, no matter what he demanded for her sexual pleasure, would be the fight. One he looked forward to. He knew Tess better than she knew herself. He knew from her father's admission of the books her mother had found, what turned her on. It wasn't the pain, it was the domination, the submission into the sexual extremes that she craved. She wanted to fight. She wanted to be vanquished, and he wanted to give it to her.

He pulled her against him, luxuriating in the warmth of her body, her very presence. He had dreamed of this for two years. He knew the moment he met Tess that she held a part of him that no other woman ever could. The thought of it had tormented him, racked him with lust. In the past months, it had grown worse. He lived and breathed daily with the need for her. It was like a fever burning his loins that he couldn't escape.

And now he had her. By Valentine's night, her final lesson, her final erotic dream fulfilled, she would know who mastered her body and her heart.

# Chapter Nine

**ဆ**

Tess was sore. Her entire body throbbed, protesting her wakefulness. The muscles of her legs were stiff and burning, her arms and even her breasts were sore.

"Open your eyes, Tess. We have to remove the plug and you need a hot bath." Cole's voice was firm, brooking no refusal.

Her eyes snapped open, her head turning to him, her eyes focusing on the savage features of his face.

"You left that thing in me?" she bit out incredulously.

He arched a single brow.

"Your ass was tight, Tess. It needs to accustom itself to stretching before you'll ever be able to take my cock there."

Her heart slammed into her ribs.

"Go to the bathroom, then come back here. If you try to remove it yourself, I'll tie you back down and leave you there the rest of the day."

He meant it. She saw his determination in the hard lines of his face.

"Take it out first," she said instead.

He shook his head. "Do as I say, Tess. I have a reason for my demands, baby."

Tess frowned, but she knew she did not want to experience the torture of being tied down and frothing with need. And she knew he would make her froth. He would torture her, then leave her to suffer in her arousal. She wasn't ready to take that chance yet, not after last night.

So she rose from the bed, walking gingerly to the bathroom. After relieving her most pressing need, she brushed her teeth and washed her face then returned to the bedroom. Her stomach rolled with nerves, wondering how Cole planned to continue the sensual torture he had started last night.

"On your knees." He nodded to the bed, standing beside it, naked and sporting an erection that resembled a weapon.

His cock was the largest she had ever seen, nearly as thick as her wrist, with a bulging, flared head that made her mouth water at the sight.

Tess went to the bed, assuming the position she knew he wanted. She trembled as his hand caressed the cheeks of her rear. His fingers ran down the crease of her ass until he gripped the plug, pulling it slowly, gently, free of her bottom.

"Stay still," he ordered her before she could move. "Under your cabinet are some personal supplies I bought for you. From now on you will use them whenever I tell you to do so. Understood?"

"Yes," she whispered, feeling her cunt burn, moisten as he ran his hands over her ass.

"I'm not going to fuck you now because to be honest, I don't think I can keep my cock out of your ass. But I need relief, baby."

He moved around the bed then, turning her as he faced her, his cock aiming at her mouth. Tess licked her lips. She opened them as the purpled head nudged against them. She heard his hard groan as she closed her lips around his cock, taking him, opening her throat to take that last inch possible.

One of his hands gripped his cock, to assure he didn't give her more than she could take, the other twisted in her hair. The sharp bite of pain had her mouth tightening around his cock, her throat working on the head as he cried out in pleasure. He wasn't willing to prolong his own pleasure this morning though. His thrust in and out of her mouth with deep, hard strokes, holding her still as he groaned repeatedly at the pleasure she was bringing him. Then, she felt his cock jerk, throb, and the pulse of his sperm filling her mouth as he cried out his release.

Cole was breathing hard when he pulled back from her, his cock was still engorged, still ready for her, but he did nothing more.

"Go bathe, Tess, before I do something neither of us is ready for. Come down to breakfast when you're finished."

Tess stood up, watching him fight for control.

"Is Father home?" she asked

"Not yet." He shook his head. "He'll be back the night before the party. You're mine until then, Tess. Can you handle it?"

Her eyes narrowed at his tone of voice, the suggestion that she couldn't.

"I can handle you any day of the week." Damn her mouth, she groaned as the words poured from her lips.

His lips quirked. They both knew better.

"We'll see." He nodded. "Go bathe. I'll lay out what I want you to wear this morning. The servants have been given the rest of the week off as well, so there's just you and me for a while."

Tess bit her lip. She wasn't certain if that was a good thing or not.

"Go." He indicated the bathroom door. "Come downstairs when you're ready."

\* \* \* \* \*

An hour later Tess walked down the spiraling stairs, barefoot and wearing more clothes than she thought he would lay out for her but decidedly less than she wanted to wear. The long, silk negligee made her feel sexy, feminine. It covered her breasts but was cut low enough that if he wanted them out, he would have no problems. There were no panties included, but the black silk shielded that fact. She would have been uncomfortable in something he could have seen right through.

His note had stated that he would await her in the kitchen, and there he was. Dressed in sweat pants and nothing else, his thick black hair still damp, looking sexier than any man had a right to look. And he was smiling at her. Even his eyes were filled with a lazy, comfortable expression as he set two plates of eggs, bacon and toast beside full coffee cups.

"Breakfast is ready, you're right on time." He pulled her chair out, indicating that she should sit.

Tess took her seat gingerly, the soreness of her muscles was much better, but her thighs and rear were still tender.

"Sore?" He brushed a kiss over her bare shoulder, causing her to jerk in startled reaction.

She turned her head, looking up at him as he straightened and moved to his own chair.

"A little." She cleared her throat.

"It will get easier," he promised. "Now eat. We'll talk later, after you've been fed."

Breakfast, despite her initial misgivings, was filled with laughter. Cole was comfortable and his easy humor began to show. His dry wit kept her chuckling and the wicked sparkle in his eyes kept her body sizzling, kept her anticipating later, praying he would fuck her. The longer he waited, the hotter she got. She didn't know if she would survive it much longer.

Finally, after the dishes were finished, he drew her through the house into the comfortable living room. A fire crackled in the corner of the room where a large, thick pillow mattress had been laid.

"Sit down, we need to talk." He drew her down on the mattress, then onto her back as he lay beside her.

"Look, I don't much feel like talking," she finally said in frustration. "Let's just cut to the chase here, Cole. There are things I evidently like, that you enjoy doing. I don't want to talk about them. Just do them."

She stared up at him, narrowing her eyes, warning him that she too had her limits.

He propped his head on his hand, regarding her with a curious expression.

"I expected more of a fight," he said, a vague question in his voice.

Tess sighed, sitting up staring into the fire as she ran the fingers of one hand through her hair.

"How extreme do you intend to get?" she finally asked him, glancing at him as he still reclined beside her.

He reached over, his fingers trailing down her hair. "How extreme do you want me to get, Tess?" he asked instead. "I can give you whatever you want, anything you want. But I have my own needs, and they will have to be satisfied as well."

"Such as?" she asked him, keeping her voice low, stilling the tremor that threatened to shake it.

"I like the toys, Tess. I like using them, and I'm dying to use them on you. I like spanking you. I like watching your pretty pussy and the rounded cheeks of your ass turning red. I like hearing you scream because you don't know if it hurts or if it's the pleasure killing you. I want to see your eyes filled with dazed pleasure as I push your limits." He laid it out for her pretty well, she thought with an edge of silent mockery, and still didn't answer a damned thing.

"How far will you go?" she asked him.

"How far will you let me go?" he countered her.

Tess had a feeling she would have few limits, but she wasn't willing to tell him that.

"You evidently have plans. I'd like to know what they are."

Cole sighed. "Some things are better left up to the pleasure of the moment. Let's wait and see what happens."

Tess licked her lips in nervousness. Evidently her father had told him about the debacle with the books her mother had found. He wouldn't have known about them otherwise. She took a deep, hard breath.

"Does it concern other men?" she finally asked.

His eyes lit up in arousal. Tess lowered her head to her knees. God, she didn't know if she could.

"You want it, Tess." He moved behind her, sitting up to pull her against him as he whispered the words in her ear. "You've wanted it for a long time, baby, everything I have planned. Just settle down, and we'll take it step by step."

Tess was fighting to control her breathing, her heart rate. She was terrified of him, and of herself.

"I can't, if Father found out—"

"Tess, your father knows," he said gently. "Why do you think your mother divorced him? She didn't want sex, let alone what he needed. Your father knew when those books were found what you needed. Just as he knows what I need."

Embarrassment coursed through her body. She remembered coming home from college, her mother raging at her, the humiliation of the accusations she had thrown at Tess. It was one of the few times her father had put his foot down. Then he had pulled her into his study and uncomfortably informed her that sexuality was a personal thing, and none of his or her mother's business.

"Your sister—?" She left the question hanging.

"Knows what he wants and enjoys it. That's the key point, Tess. You have to enjoy it, otherwise, it brings me no pleasure. Your pleasure is most important, Tess. What you want, what you need."

His hands were at her abdomen, softly stroking the nervous muscles there. His lips brushed over her shoulder, her neck.

"I don't want a toy, Tess," he promised her. "Or a woman who doesn't know her mind and speak up accordingly. But in the bedroom, that is where I want the woman I know you are. If you want to fight me, then fight. If you want to submit, then do so. If you want to be tied down and raped, let me know. All of it, I can give you and enjoy. But if you ever reach a limit, you have to tell me. If I ever suggest something you don't want or can't handle, then you have to speak up. And after that, unless you ask for it, it will never be approached again. So be very careful in the pleasures you deny yourself."

She lifted her head from her knees.

"And when you're tired of me?" she asked him.

"What if you grow tired of me first?" he asked her then. "It goes both ways, Tess. If we can't give the other what they need, then there's no point in going on. Do you agree?"

Her hands clenched at her knees. "I agree," she whispered.

"There are no rules, Tess. But from this point on, no means no. If you don't want it, then you say the word. Understand?"

She nodded nervously.

"Each night, I'll push you further. Each night, you'll learn something new about yourself." His hands moved to her arms, caressing the tight muscles, easing the nervousness locking them up. "Don't be frightened of me, Tess. Or of yourself."

"No other women." She wanted it clear from the beginning. "I don't know if I can even handle another man. But you can have no other women."

"I don't want another woman, Tess," he assured her. "And there will be no other men, unless it's something I decide." His voice hardened. "There is a particular pleasure in sharing your woman that you may never understand. But not just any man would be worthy of the privilege, baby, trust me."

"If you don't fuck me now, I'll walk out of this house and I won't come back," she finally breathed roughly. "I'm tired of waiting, Cole."

She had turned the tables on him then, she moved before he could stop her, turning and pressing against his shoulders until he lay back on the mattress. He was already hard, and she was already wet. His cock tented the front of his pants, hiding him from her. Hooking her hands in the waistband she pulled them down, lifting them over the thick erection and jerking them from his legs.

"I wondered when you would get tired of waiting," he said with a smile, though his gaze was hot, wickedly lustful.

Tess jerked the gown over her head, then moved up his body. She heard his hard breath when her damp cunt grazed his cock, but she continued on. She wanted his kiss. She was dying for it.

As her lips touched his, his arms went around her, turning her, flipping her onto her back as he rose above her. His tongue pierced her mouth, his lips slanting over hers as he turned the caress into a carnal feast. Tess moaned brokenly, feeling the tenderness, the utter warmth of his touch, his body above hers, the easy strength of his muscles as he kept her close against him.

"My dick is so hard I won't last five minutes inside you," he bit out. "Are you on the pill, or do I need a condom?"

"Pill," she gasped. She didn't want anything between them. She wanted to feel him when he came, feel his seed spurting hard inside her.

"Damn, Tess, I'm almost scared to fuck you, you're so damned tight," he growled as his hand smoothed over her cunt, his finger testing her vagina.

Tess arched into the penetration, her hungry moan shocking her as her body begged for more.

His lips trailed along her neck, moving steadily down, down to the hard, sensitive tips of her breasts. When his mouth covered one, her womb contracted painfully. Oh yeah. That was good. SO good. His tongue rasped over the tip, his mouth suckling at her with a strong motion that left her quivering. Then he nibbled at the small bud, the slight pinch driving her arousal higher with the edge of pain.

"Damn, you're so hot you're burning me alive," he growled, moving back to her lips, searing them with his kiss.

"Burn more then," she panted. "Please, Cole. Take me now."

He rose above her moving between her thighs, spreading them wide, as she watched his cock pulse.

"It might hurt," he warned her, breathing heavy. "Damn, Tess, I've never had a pussy so tight it burned my finger before."

She rolled her hips, tormented by the tip of his cock as it nudged against her vagina.

"That's okay," she whimpered. " You can handle it."

He surged inside her.

The breath left Tess's body as it bowed, a strangled scream tearing from her throat at the forced separation of her sensitive vaginal muscles. The burning pleasure/pain consumed her, traveling through her as she twisted against the thick cock lodged in her cunt.

"Sweet mercy, Tess," Cole cried out as he came over her heavily, his elbows bracing to take his weight. His hips rolled in a smooth motion between her thighs that sent sharp darts of ecstasy traveling through her body.

* * * * *

He wasn't going to last long. Cole knew he didn't have a prayer of it. The best he could hope for was that Tess wouldn't either. He grabbed her hips, his face buried in the damp curve of her neck as he began a strong steady motion inside her body.

Her cunt was so tight it burned, so slick and sweet he could stay inside her forever if only he could hold his release back that long. There wasn't a chance. She twisted against him, her hips lifting for him, her legs wrapping around his waist as she took him deeper, screaming out with the sensations his hard thrusts sent through her.

Cole groaned at her heat. He pushed into her harder, his thrusts gaining in speed, spearing inside her, sliding through sensitive tissue that gripped him, fought to hold him. Her body tightened further until finally, her pussy began to quake around him as she cried out, jerking in his arms, her orgasm slamming into her at the same time he lost control.

Cole heard his howl of ecstasy, her strangled scream of release as he began spurting inside her. Heat enveloped him, seared him, filled his body and soul as her hold on him tightened.

"Tess. God, Tess, baby—" He didn't think the hard flares of pleasure would ever end. Prayed they never did. They shot up his spine, through his dick, and dissolved the hard, lonely core to his heart. This woman was his. And before the week was over, he would prove it to her.

# Chapter Ten

ରେ

For Tess, the days continued in a haze of pleasure. Cole was alternately gentle and masterful, seductive and surprising. He pushed her as he warned he would. He tied her down and tormented her with his skillful tongue and a variety of sexual toys meant to both tease and torment. Throughout the day she wore the silky gowns he laid out for her, and roamed the house with him. They talked and laughed, made love and lust in a variety of rooms and positions. But more importantly, Tess learned about the man.

The privileged, driven man whose incredible intelligence often hid a man of intense emotions. She would catch glimpses of it during certain conversations or after a session of intense, almost brutal lovemaking. His expression would be concerned, loving, as though despite his needs, his desires, he feared hurting her.

He still made her wear the butt plug for several hours daily. Before it was time to remove it, he would fuck her slow and easy, his cock sliding forcefully inside the ultra tight passage of her vagina. The sensation was incredible. Tess would scream for him, beg, plead for mercy as the streaking pain and pleasure assaulted her body. Her climaxes tore her body apart with the sensations, leaving her heaving against him, her juices exploding around his cock and triggering his own climax.

Their time was slowly coming to a close, though. On the sixth day, Tess dressed in yet another gown. The new one was a Grecian design that fell to her feet, with small golden silken ropes crossing over the front from her abdomen to beneath her breasts. She was barefoot again, but she knew that Cole would be as well. He wore clothes easy to remove. She grinned. For the most part, they went naked through the house anyway.

They went through breakfast quickly. Tess knew Cole had something planned for the day, but she wasn't certain what. She learned quickly a bit later, though. As she lay on the mattress in front of the fire Cole pulled four massively heavy weights from the corner of the room. He placed one at each corner of the mattress, then gave her that dark, commanding look that set her blood on fire.

"Last lesson," he whispered, tying a length of silken rope on the metal rings wielded to them.

"Take off your gown and lay on your stomach."

A tremor of arousal shook her body as she pulled the gown from her body. Cole then buckled a leather band at each ankle and wrist before attaching the ropes to them. It left her spread, defenseless, with just enough play in the rope for him to place large, wide pillows beneath her body, levering her several inches above the mattress. Under her hips he placed yet another, leaving her ass defenseless, open to his gaze.

"Who owns your body?" he whispered, running his finger along the flaming crease of her cunt as his other hand stroked her buttocks.

"I do." Her voice was rough. She was in the right position for punishment; she didn't want to waste it.

His hand landed on her ass with stinging force. She flinched, cried out at the flare of heat in her flesh and deep within her cunt.

"Who owns your body, Tess?" he asked her again.

"Not you," she cried out. She needed more, again. She wanted him to set her ass to burning, because she knew what it would do to the rest of her body. Her breasts were swollen, her nipples hard and hurting.

He slapped her again.

"Who owns your body?"

191

"Me." The haze of arousal was dulling reality now. His hand landed again.

"Need any help, Cole?" For a moment, Tess thought she imagined the smooth, cultured voice coming from the doorway.

She opened her eyes, her head turning, her eyes widening in mortification at the man leaning casually against the doorframe.

Jesse Wyman was one of the vice presidents at her father's company, answerable only to Cole and her father. He was as darkly handsome as Cole was, but more refined, not as large or savage looking. His green eyes were dark now, filled with lust rather than calculation, and the bulge in his pants looked more than impressive.

"Cole?" Was this part of his plan, if not, her suddenly dripping pussy may just get her into trouble.

"Say no and he walks away." Cole's voice was hot, suggestive. "Do you remember the book your mother threw the biggest fit over, Tess?" he whispered hotly. "The woman was tied down, her ass raised, her cunt, her mouth and her ass at the mercy of the hero and his best friend? Meet my best friend, baby."

Tess quivered. She could feel Cole's hand stroking over her heated bottom, Jesse's eyes following the caress. Her heart labored heavily in excitement, the blood thundering through her veins. She had always wondered what it would feel like. Wondered if she could handle two men at once.

"Cole—?" She was frightened too. The unfamiliar longings were shuttling through her body, making her shake in indecision.

"Tess, " he whispered. "It won't be the last time I ask it of you. I promise you, baby, you'll love it."

She could hear the excitement in his voice, the arousal as Jesse started into the room, his hands going to the buttons of his white dress shirt.

"God, you two do this all the time?" she gasped.

"Just sometimes. Just when it's important, Tess. When we know it's needed. And baby, you need it." His finger dipped into her pussy, pushing through the frothing juice that dripped from it.

Tess groaned, pushing back into his finger as Jesse dropped his shirt to the floor. His chest was muscular and deeply tanned. His green eyes glittering with rising lust. Tess watched, mesmerized as his hand went to the fastening of his slacks.

"She's beautiful," Jesse growled as he kicked his shoes off then disposed of his slacks and boxers. "Has she been a good girl for you, Cole?" His voice was suggestive, searing her with the implication that she needed to be punished.

His hands tested the restraints at her wrists, then his fingers feathered over her cheek. Tess shuddered at the caress.

"Tess usually finds a way to be naughty, don't you, baby?" Cole's hand landed on her bottom in a light smack.

She jerked, whimpering. Dear God, they were both going to punish her, pleasure her? She felt faint from excitement, her body tingling. She nearly climaxed when Jesse came to his knees beside her, his erection not as large as Cole's, but nearly. It was thick, pulsing, the head throbbing. His hand touched her hair, his eyes locked with hers, and then Tess understood why Cole had propped pillows beneath her whole body. To raise her high enough to keep her arms stretched wide, and still in position for any cock sucking required. Her mouth watered at the thought, then opened in a cry of surprise when Cole's hand struck her ass again.

"Naughty Tess." His voice was filled with amusement.

"Beautiful Tess," Jesse's voice was a low growl of pleasure. "Her butt pinkens so well. Does it stretch as easily?"

"My ass," Cole grunted. "I haven't fucked it yet, so you can't either."

193

Jesse grunted but said nothing more. A second later, Tess felt his lips at her shoulder, his teeth scraping over her skin as his hands reached beneath her on either side to cup her full, swollen breasts. His fingers gripped her nipples, pinching lightly as she groaned at the hot little flare of pain. She jerked at the caress, fighting to breathe as she felt Cole's hand descend on her ass once again. She was bucking at each blow, crying out as Jesse alternately soothed and inflamed her nipples, his mouth on her neck, nibbling, licking at her, keeping her poised on a pinnacle of arousal so sharp it was agony.

It was then that Tess felt Cole move away from her for a second. When he returned, his finger, thickly lubricated, began to work its way up her still tight anus. He slid the first in easily, though her muscles pinched at the entrance. He pulled back slowly, then two broad fingers were working up the tight channel, spreading her, thrusting lightly inside as she cried out, begging for more.

Jesse's fingers tightened on her nipples, then caressed them, tightened again, caressed again. Cole's fingers, three now, worked slowly up her small back entrance, his voice hot and encouraging as she opened to him, her muscles stretching as it sent fire flaring through her body.

"I'm going to fuck your ass today, Tess," he growled. "I'm going to lubricate you real good, baby, then I'm going to work my cock up your tight ass and listen to you scream for me. Will you scream for me, baby?"

Scream? She couldn't breathe. She was gasping for breath as Jesse pulled the pillows from beneath her body, lying down beside her, his strong arms holding her up as he pushed his head under her to catch a hard, turgid nipple in his mouth.

There was enough slack to the ropes holding her wrists now that she could partially prop herself up with her hands. Jesse helped her hold her weight, splayed as she was, with his hard hands beneath her breasts. But did little for her strength.

The strong suction, strong nips and rasping tongue on her tender nipples were driving her crazy.

Her head tossed as she panted for breath. Cole's fingers were working further up her ass now, spilling fire and hot, dark rapture as he slowly stretched her, his fingers spreading inside her to part the heated passage.

"Jesse is going to fuck your tight pussy for me, Tess," Cole promised her, his voice rough from his lust. "After I work my cock up your sweet ass, he's going to take that tight cunt. You'll be stretched and full baby, both of us working you, fucking you."

His explicit words caused her womb to spasm painfully, her body to bow involuntarily as she pushed against his fingers.

"Oh yes, baby, you want it, don't you?" Pleasure filled his voice. "You want to be taken, filled and fucked like the sweet treasure you are."

His voice was awed, enraptured, as though it were she giving him a gift, rather than the other way around. As Cole spoke, Jesse pushed his body beneath hers, sliding easily in the space the cushions had once taken until she was draped over him, his cock nestling at the soaked lips of her bare cunt.

"Tess, I wish you could see how beautiful you look," Cole groaned as he moved back until Jesse could get into position. "Your sweet cunt is dripping all over his cock, soaking it. Your ass raised and ready for me. Are you ready for me, baby?"

Tess whimpered. Was she ready? The thought of his cock, so thick and hard pushing up her ass was at once terrifying and exhilarating.

"I think you're ready." She felt him move into position as Jesse reached around, pulling the cheeks of her ass apart.

"Relax for me, Tess," Cole groaned. "I promise, it's gonna be so good."

She felt the head of his cock begin its entrance inside her. Slowly, easing inside her, stretching her until she was screaming out at the shocking pain of the entrance. Pain and pleasure, it seared her, held her immobile as he worked his cock inside her, inch by inch.

Jesse held her flesh apart, but his lips caressed her face, whispering encouragement, dark, naughty words that made her need for the sexual pain flare higher, hotter. His voice was approving, tender.

"It's okay, Tess," he soothed her as she bucked, her eyes tearing from the pain, though she didn't want it to stop. She never wanted it to stop. "Don't fight it, Tess," he urged. "Cole's cock is thick, baby, but not too thick. You can take it." He pulled her flesh apart further, easing the shocking pain as Cole continued to tunnel inside her.

"Tess, are you okay, baby?" She could hear the strain in his voice, the hot vibrating vein of lust and possession, caring and tenderness.

"Please—" she gasped as he halted the slow, gliding entrance.

The head of his cock had just passed the tight ring of muscles, the flared tip stretching it wide as she fought to accustom herself to his large cock filling her there.

"More, baby?" he asked her, his hand smoothing down her back.

"More," she cried, her hips easing back on the burning lance. "More. Please, Cole. More."

He began to ease further inside her as the tip of Jesse's cock throbbed at the entrance to her cunt. A slow, steady stroke had Cole filling her ass completely, his hard groan as he sank into her to his balls echoed in the room.

Tess was crying out repeatedly now, her muscles clenching on him, her body accepting the pain as a torturous pleasure she couldn't deny any longer. Her hips moved against him, driving him deeper, lodging the pulsing head of Jesse's cock just inside her vaginal entrance as Cole pulled back, then pushed forward again.

"Yes," she screamed out as he began an easy thrusting motion inside her ass. "Oh God, Cole. Fuck me. Please fuck me!"

He pushed harder inside her. Once. Twice. Then stilled. Tess would have protested, but she lost her breath. Beneath her, Jesse began to push his hard cock into the tiny, tiny entrance of her vagina. Cole's cock filled her ass to bursting, leaving little room in her snug pussy. But Jesse didn't let that hinder him. Groaning, praising the ultra tight fit, he sank slowly into the heated depths until he was lodged in to the hilt.

Reality ceased to exist. She didn't even know when Jesse had reached up to release the leather manacles or when Cole had released those at her ankles. But she was on her hands and knees, sandwiched between them, begging for more. Pleading for the hard thrusts of their cocks inside her as they set up a slow, rhythmic thrusting motion that threatened to drown her in pleasure. She was insane with the burning ecstasy spearing her body. She moved against them, taking them, urging them on until their building thrusts were powerful strokes inside her. They were fucking her hard and fast now, each man groaning, praising her, crying out as she tightened on them.

"Cole," she screamed out his name as she felt her orgasm building. "Oh God, Cole, I can't stand it."

"You can, Tess," he groaned, levering over her body as his hips powered inside her. "You can, baby. Take it. Take it, Tess. Cum for me, baby. Cum for me now." He surged inside her as she tightened around him.

Beneath her, Jesse had clasped her waist hard, his hips slamming into hers, and despite their speed, both men kept in perfect synchronization with the hard thrusts of their cocks inside her body.

Tess couldn't stop her screams, couldn't stop the sensations that tightened her body, the boiling pressure, the hard, piercing pleasure/pain was too much for her untutored body to take for long. When she climaxed, she wailed out at the explosion, tightening on them further, her ass, her cunt milking the cocks possessing her until she heard their shattered male groans and felt the hard, spurting jets of their sperm filling each hole.

Her orgasm shuddered through her body, over and over. Her muscles clenched on their cocks as they exploded inside her, making them cry out around her, jerk against her as her cunt and her ass drew on their flesh, shuddered around it, burned them with her release until she fell against Jesse gasping, boneless.

"Son of a bitch, Cole," Jesse's voice was harsh, weary now. "She's drained me."

Cole pulled free of her and collapsed on the mattress, helping Jesse to lower Tess between them. Once there, he pulled her against his body, his hands running over her back, his lips caressing her temple as she fought to regain her breath.

"You're mine, Tess," he whispered, stopping her heart with the emotion she heard in his voice. "Taken by me. Held by me. I won't let you escape me again."

She would have answered him, but shock held her immobile when she heard the enraged scream of her mother from the doorway.

"You dirty whore! Just like your father. You're just like your father—!"

# Chapter Eleven

#### ১৩

"Oh my God!" Humiliation sped through Tess's system seconds later as Cole and Jesse jumped to hide her from sight.

They jerked their pants from the floor, shielding Tess as they dressed quickly. Cole's body was tight with fury as Tess fumbled with her gown, her fingers shaking so badly she could barely get it over her head.

Turning to her, still shielding her, Cole helped her untangle the material and ease it over her head.

"I'm sorry, baby," he whispered, his lips feathering over her hair as he straightened the gown.

Tess shook her head, feeling the heat that traveled over her face. With a final touch of his fingertips to her cheek, he turned to her mother.

"How the hell did you get in?" His voice was furious as he faced Ella Delacourte, dark and warning.

"I didn't come here to talk to you, perverted bastard that you are. Look how you corrupted my daughter. You're just like that trashy, home wrecking sister of yours." Ella was screeching now.

Tess felt her face flame in shame as she stood to her feet, her legs shaking from her exertions and her fear. Dear God, how had her mother got into the house?

"Mother, why are you here?" Tess's voice was thick with tears and confusion.

She wasn't ashamed that she had experienced the sexuality of the act. But being caught in it was mortifying. And by her mother!

"I came to see why you were here after I found out your father and his tramp were away for the week," she sneered. "You haven't even called me. I was worried."

The classic guilt trip from her mother any time Tess spent time with her father.

"Ella, control your tongue," Jesse's voice was hard and laced with warning.

Tess looked at him in surprise. She had no idea Jesse knew her mother.

Ella cast the other man a look that should have withered him with shame. Jesse stood before her, his shoulders squared, his dark face furious.

"Tess, go shower or something." Cole drew her into his arms, kissing her head softly, his hands soothing on her back. "Let me take care of this."

Tess shook her head.

"I haven't needed you to fight my battles before this, Cole. I don't need you to do it now," she said. "I haven't done anything wrong—"

"Wrong?" Ella's voice was piercing. "You think fucking your perverted lover and his friend isn't wrong, Tess? I raised you better than to whore for some depraved bastard."

Tess trembled at the fury in her mother's voice.

"Ella!" Jesse's voice was a lash of cold, hard fury now. "Get the hell out of here before I escort you out. And I don't think you want me to have to do that."

The heated edge of fury in Jesse's voice surprised Tess.

"Get her the hell out of here," Cole muttered to his friend.

"Would you guys just stop this?" Tess ran her fingers through her hair, hating the tremble in her hands as she faced her mother.

Years of being made to feel ashamed of her sexuality, of her needs as a woman washed over her. She remembered the lectures from the time she was a child, on the depravities of sex and the sins of the flesh.

"Mother, I told you I'd be back after the party," she sighed, leaning against Cole for support, thankful in a way that she didn't have to hide from her mother now.

"How could you do this, Tess?" Ella's expression was livid, her gray eyes glittering with fury. "How could you have become so depraved?"

"Depraved?" Tess shook her head, sighing. "I'm just different from you. I'm sorry."

A tear escaped her eyes. She hated having her mother angry with her, just as she had hated leaving her father so long ago.

As she finished speaking, a movement behind her mother caught Tess's attention. Her father, tall and strong, his face coldly furious, moved into the room.

"Well, I guess you're satisfied," Ella sneered when she saw him. "She's just like you and that whore you married."

Missy was with her father, and for once, Tess saw anger lining the beautiful blonde's face.

"You're in my home, Ella," Missy reminded her, her slender body tense and lined with anger. "I suggest you leave it and consider what you're losing in this display you seem intent on. Tess isn't a child. She's a woman. Her lifestyle is none of your concern."

Fury pulsed through the room, nearly choking Tess.

"I can't believe you did this. That a child of mine would lower herself to the same games her father plays." Tess flinched under the cold, unrelenting judgment her mother was meting out.

"Ella!" Missy's voice was a lash of hot fury. "I will have you escorted from my home if you cannot speak to your daughter decently. What she does is no business of yours. She's a grown woman."

"And I don't need anyone fighting my battles for me," Tess bit out, more than surprised at the confident edge of power in her stepmother's voice. Missy with a backbone? She wouldn't have believed it.

"Do you know what she was doing here, Jason?" Ella screamed out at her ex-husband. "This had gone even further than the games you practice—"

"For God's sake, Ella!" Jason cursed furiously. "Listen to you. Do you think our daughter wants to hear this? Our problems don't involve her." Her father's face was ruddy with his own embarrassment. "I don't care what she was doing. I trust Cole to protect her, that's all I needed to know."

"Well had you shown up a moment sooner—"

"Then I would have warned them of my arrival before entering the house," he growled in disgust as he cast Tess an apologetic look. "For pity's sake, stop humiliating Tess because of your own bitterness. This has gone too far."

Ella turned to Tess, her eyes hard, resentful. "Leave your belongings, Tess. You're going home with me. Now!"

When had she ever given her mother permission to order her around in such a manner? Tess watched her in growing confusion and pain. She had never known how angry, how bitter her mother had become. And for what reason? She had often stated how her life was more secure without a man interfering in it.

"I won't leave, Mother." She felt Cole's hands tighten at her shoulders, the way his body tensed expectantly behind her.

Shock filled her mother's expression.

"What did you say?" She seemed to gasp.

"I won't leave—"

"He's using you, Tess," Ella said furiously. "You'll be nothing but his whore. He proved that today."

Tess shook her head. "I love him, Mother. I have for years and I was too scared to admit to it. But I'm even more frightened of being alone and bitter, without at least having this time with him."

Silence held the room. She thought she heard Cole whisper a reverent "Thank God." But she wasn't certain.

"You will," Ella screamed furiously, her fists clenching at her side, her eyes glittering wildly. "You won't stay with these monsters."

"Perhaps it's where I belong." Tess wanted to cry out at the hurt that flashed in her mother's eyes. "I love Cole, Mother, and I'm not ashamed of that, or what I've done. I enjoyed it."

Ella opened her mouth to say more.

"Don't speak, Ella," Jason snapped. "Keep your mouth shut and leave her the hell alone."

"You don't control me, Jason," Ella bit out, her body trembling. "You didn't while we were married and you don't now."

"Probably what her problem is," Cole whispered at Tess's ear.

Her eyes widened for a moment before she put her elbow in his hard stomach. He only chuckled.

"I will if you don't keep that viperous tongue quiet," he growled. "And trust me, Ella, you better be careful. You may find out the monsters you hate so much are more a part of you than you know."

"I'm not part of this," Jesse finally sighed as he finished dressing. "I'm heading out of here, boys and girls. See you at the office, Cole."

He slapped Cole on the shoulder before leaving the room.

Ella's eyes followed him, narrowed, furious.

"Mother, perhaps you should leave as well." Tess took a hard, deep breath. "We'll discuss this later, when we're both calmer."

Ella turned back to her. The perfectly groomed cap of auburn hair framed a surprisingly young face. At forty-two, Ella Delacourte looked nearly a decade younger. But she was more bitter and vengeful than any woman twice her age, with a much harder life. "Come with me now, Tess, or I won't allow you back in my home." Ella's lips thinned as she stared at her daughter, ice coating her voice. "You'll no longer be a daughter of mine."

Tess trembled. She had never seen her mother so angry.

"I'm sorry, Mother." She shook her head. "I can't."

Ella drew herself erect. She cast her ex-husband a dark look then turned and stalked from the house. Tess flinched as the front door slammed closed behind her.

"She'll settle down, Tess," Jason said gently. "You know how your mother gets."

Tess ran her fingers through her hair as she took a hard, deep breath.

"She won't forgive me, Father," she said, her voice low, thick with tears. "Not ever. No more than she ever forgave you."

"Tess," Cole's voice was soft, gentle as his arms wrapped around her, holding her.

What a perfect feeling, she thought, to be held so tight, so warm against him. But how long would it last? How long could it last? She loved him, but how could he love her? Had her own desires, her unnatural needs lost her the love of the only man she had ever truly wanted?

# Chapter Twelve

ℒ

The question followed Tess through the rest of that night. Cole didn't come to her bed. For the first time in six nights, he wasn't beside her, tempting her, teasing her with his body, his lust. She lay in the middle of the big bed, staring silently up at the vaulted ceiling, the loneliness of the room smothering her. God help her, if she couldn't get through one night without him, how would she handle the rest of her life?

What had she done? Had her desire to experience with him everything his other women had been her downfall? Had her envy, her depravity, ruined the only chance she had to make him love her? She swallowed the tight knot of fear in her throat. Realistically, she had known that her chances of capturing his heart were slim. She just hadn't expected it to be over so soon.

Realizing she wouldn't be sleeping any time soon, Tess got up, pulling on the bronzed silk robe that lay at the bottom of the bed and belting it firmly. She slipped her feet into soft, matching slippers and left the room. She would prefer to sit in the kitchen, drowning her sorrows in the chocolate mint ice cream her father kept on hand, rather than wallowing in them.

As she stepped into the hallway, she followed the bright light spilling from the kitchen further up the hall. She halted in surprise at the doorway. Dressed in a thick robe, her blonde hair attractively mussed, her surprisingly pretty face free of makeup, sat Missy, digging into a bowl of the mint flavored chocolate, the box sitting temptingly in front of her.

"Great minds think alike?" Missy flashed her a smile as she looked up, waving the spoon in her hand at the cabinet. "Grab a bowl."

Tess walked to the cabinet and did just that, then sat down at the other side of the rounded table and began to spoon in a large portion.

"Nothing settles the nerves like Chocolate Mint," Missy sighed. "And I guess today rates as definitely that."

"I'm sorry," Tess apologized, genuinely regretful that she had caused her stepmother any pain. "I didn't expect Mother to show up."

Missy paused, her spoon suspended above her bowl as she flashed Tess a frown.

"Tess, I'm not upset for me," she said sincerely. "I'm upset for you and Cole. Your private choices should not be aired in such a manner. Cole was furious, of course, that she hurt you. But I was angry for your sake."

"Why?" Tess frowned. "We've never been close. We barely get along."

A knowing smile tipped Missy's pale lips.

"Tess, you fight with someone when you feel threatened, and when you care without a safety net, an assurance that you are cared for as well. I know that. I used to be the same way, until I met Jace."

Tess hunched her shoulders. Missy's assessment was much too close to the truth.

"That's how I knew you loved Cole." Missy dropped her next bombshell. "At first, it was just general sniping, but as he teased and flirted and pushed you, it became outright fighting on your side. I knew then your heart was involved."

Tess nearly choked on the spoonful of ice cream she was attempting to swallow. How could anyone, especially airhead Missy, who wasn't such an airhead after all, know her better than she knew herself?

"Have I lost him?" Tess couldn't keep the longing, the fear from her voice as she stared back at the other woman.

"Lost Cole?" Missy laughed in surprising amusement. "Tess, Cole has been fighting for your attention for over two years now. What the future will bring, I don't know. But I sincerely doubt you have anything to worry about for the present."

This did little ease to her worry.

"He hasn't returned." She shrugged, dropping her eyes to her bowl. "Maybe I disgusted him. Maybe I was supposed to refuse when Jesse came in?"

When Missy didn't answer, Tess risked a quick look.

The other woman watched her sympathetically, warmly.

"Cole is different from other men," she said as Tess watched her worriedly. "How different, is up to you to discover. But I've known him all his life, and I know Cole doesn't play games. If he invited Jesse, then he wanted it too. He wouldn't try to trap you, Tess, or hurt you. You have to trust him that far."

"I'm scared," Tess admitted, her eyes going back to the melting ice cream. "I don't know how to handle what I feel and what I want."

"Do any of us?" Missy's chuckle was self-mocking. "It takes meeting the man who can give us what we need, who knows, because it's what they need. I know, Tess, because that's what your father and I have. A relationship that fulfills what both of us need."

"Mother never loved him." Tess knew that, had known it for a long time.

"Your mother has to love herself first." Missy shrugged. "Now finish your ice cream. I'm sure Cole will be back before the party tomorrow, and he'll show you then how much he's missed you. I know he didn't want to leave and he hated going before talking to you first, but in this case, he assured me it was necessary."

What, Tess wondered, could have been so important that he couldn't even see her before leaving?

* * * * *

Tess waited, and she waited. All through the next day, while she was dressing for the party, and halfway through the boisterous, noisy affair she waited, and held onto the hope that he would be back that night. She gave up at nine. She set aside her glass of champagne, put away her hope and walked regally from the noisy ballroom and up the narrow steps that led to the Turret Room. She would pack and leave in the morning. She wasn't certain where she would go, but she was certain she couldn't risk staying here, or begging him to forgive her for something she didn't know if she would change.

The sexual dominance of the act had thrilled her. The utter thick, hot pleasure in Cole's voice had only spurred her on. She didn't know if it was something she would ever want again, but she knew experiencing it would be a memory she would always hold onto.

She kept her head down as she entered the room, going straight for the suitcase stored in the large walk-in closet just inside the room. She placed it on the luggage rack, opened it and re-entered the closet to collect the few things she had brought with her.

As she folded the articles of clothing, the tears began to fall. They were hot, blistering with pain, and shook her body as she tried to console herself that at least she had tried. For one time in her life, a very brief time, she was free.

She wiped at the tears, her breath hitching as she moved to the stone dresser and collect the clothing there, then she went to her bed and picked up her robe. The last article Cole had given her. It was then she saw the small, black velvet jewelers box. She stopped, clutching the silk robe to her chest

It was a ring. The diamond glittered with shards of blue and orange, intensifying the gold of the thick, simple band. Her hands shook, her body trembled. Her head raised, her eyes going to the shadows of the opened bathroom door.

"Shame on you, Tess," Cole chided her gently as he walked from the room where he waited. "To think I wouldn't come back. I'll have to punish you for that."

His chest was bare, his jeans rode low on his hips and fitted tightly over the bulge beneath the material.

Tess took a deep, hard breath.

"You didn't call," she whispered as she saw the mask of cool determination on his face, the sparkle of warmth in his eyes that was so at odds with his expression. "You didn't say goodbye."

"If I had seen you, I wouldn't have left. And I had to leave or miss the jeweler before he left. You should have known I had a reason."

Cole's voice was cool, disapproving. His eyes were patient, wicked and warm. God, she could feel her cunt heating to lava temperature.

"You knew I would worry," she snapped out, ignoring the hope, the happiness surging inside her.

"Worry, not have so little faith in me." There was an edge of hurt in his voice now, as though her tears, and the cause for them, pricked at his emotions. "After taking you, did you think I would let you go easily?"

A sob broke in her chest, another tear fell.

"I enjoyed it," she whispered brokenly. "You shouldn't love me."

"Tess," he whispered her name gently. "Don't you think I want it too? That I didn't enjoy your pleasure as well? It was the first time, baby, and it won't be the last time. I love hearing your cries, feeling your pleasure, knowing you're dominated, submitting to me, no matter what I want. Tess, I love you more for it, not less."

"How?" she whispered brokenly, shaking her head. "How could you?"

"Do you want Jesse alone, Tess?" he asked her carefully. "Would you let him touch you, hold you, if I didn't ask you to do so?"

"No!" she burst out, realizing the idea was abhorrent to her. What she had done with Cole could never have been done without him.

He came closer to her, standing within inches of her, staring down at her with heated arousal, and something more. Something she was terrified to admit to seeing. What if she was wrong? What if it wasn't love she saw in his eyes?

Rather than taking her in his arms, he indicated to her to sit on the bed. Tess did so slowly as he reached around her and retrieved the box on the bed. As her eyes rounded in shock, he went to one knee before her, holding the box in front of her as he stared up at her in adoration.

"You're mine." He wasn't asking her anything. "Taken by me, Tess. Mine to hold and mine to love now."

He took the ring from the box, picked up her hand and slid the diamond over her finger firmly.

"Is this a proposal?" she asked huskily, incredulously.

"Hell no. I'm not asking you anything," he grunted. "With that smart assed mouth of yours, you'd have me tying you down rather than loving you the way I want to."

"Loving me?" she whispered as he pushed her down on the bed, following her with his heated, hard body.

"Loving you, Tess," he promised. "With everything I have. With all I am, I love you."

His lips covered hers, his tongue pushing past her lips with a determination, a heat she couldn't deny. Her hands grasped his shoulders, her body arching to him as she groaned into the kiss. His lips ate at hers, his tongue plundering her mouth wickedly as his hands worked behind her back at the zipper of her dress, then stripped it quickly from her body.

He never broke the kiss, or lost the heat of his arousal as he stripped his pants from his hips, kicking them from his muscular legs. He didn't miss a beat as he ripped the silk of her panties from her body.

"Mine," he growled as his head finally raised, only to rake down her neck in a fiery caress, his tongue licking at her skin, his hands lifting her against him as they arrowed to her breast. There, his lips covered a hard, engorged nipple, sucking it into his mouth with a groan of arousal.

Tess arched to him, crying out brokenly at the fierce thrust of pleasure that clenched her womb and her vagina at the same time. Like a punch of heated ecstasy, her body bowed as he nibbled at the hard little point, his hand smoothing down her abdomen, his fingers parting the lips of her sex.

"Cole. Cole, please." She was on fire, needing his touch now more than she ever had.

"Say yes," he growled as his lips moved down her body, his tongue licking sensually, then his teeth nibbling with fierce, hot nips as he parted her thighs.

"Yes," she moaned, arching against him. "Yes, Cole. Anything. Just please don't stop."

He licked a slow, long stroke through the shallow valley of her cunt, his appreciation voiced in a low, long rumbling moan. His fingers parted her, his lips covered her clit with a heated suction that had her hips jerking sharply, arching to his mouth. Her knees bent, her thighs clenching around his head as he sucked and licked at the little pearl of nerves that throbbed almost painfully.

"So good," he growled, licking at her. "Delicious, Tess. But I need more, baby. Come for me. Come for me so I can love you the way I need to."

A finger, thick and long slid deep into her vagina, his mouth covered her clit, his tongue flickering in a wicked dance of pleasure as his finger filled her, retreated, then thrust inside her again. Tess bucked against him, her legs tightening around his head, her body heaving. Fire struck her loins, swelled her clit further, clenched her womb. The blood rushed through her body, carrying ecstasy, rapture, until she felt every particle of her being erupt against his mouth.

She was still crying, arching when he jerked her thighs apart and moved between them quickly.

"I love you, Tess," he whispered as he lowered himself against her, his cock, sliding against the lips of her sex, nudging inside them, then parting the tight muscles of her vagina.

"I love you," she whispered in return as the head of his cock parted her, slid in inch by inch, easing past the sensitive tissue, allowing her to feel every hard, hot, throbbing inch he was giving her. "Oh God, Cole, you'll kill me."

It was too much. He was too slow. The exquisite stretching, the slow stroke across nerve endings so sensitive, so desperate for relief, was taking her breath. Her head tossed on the bed, her hands slid across his sweat-dampened shoulders, then clenched in the silk of his hair.

"I'm loving you," he groaned. "Enjoy it, baby, it may not happen like this again for a while."

Torturous pleasure raged through her body. She could feel the clench of her vagina on the thick, hot shaft working gently inside her, the slow stretching, the hot brand of possession as he slid in to the hilt, then paused.

"Tess, baby," he whispered as he filled her, burying his face in her neck, his lips stroking her heatedly as he groaned.

She tightened the muscles of her vagina around his cock, whimpering at the heat, the searing sensations of near orgasm.

"I love you," she cried out again, holding him close, holding him tight. "I love you Cole, but I swear to God, if you don't fuck me right now, I'll kill you."

He didn't need a second urging. Bracing his knees on the mattress, he pulled back then slammed inside her. Tess screamed out at the rocketing, agonizing pleasure. Her back bowed, her legs curled around his hips, enclosing him in a vice as she fought to make him move harder, faster. She didn't have to urge him much.

With a harsh male cry of victory he began to thrust heatedly, heavily inside the slick heat of her body. Tess trembled at the onslaught of fiery sensations. Her vagina was stretched, filled, repeatedly stroked in hard, long thrusts that drove her higher, closer, strangling the breath in her throat as her release began to tear through her.

Like an orgasmic quake it rushed over her body, tightened her muscles and flung her from a precipice of agonizing need. Her cry echoed around her, distant, dazed as Cole gave one more gasping thrust then groaned out his release. She felt the hot, thick jets of his semen spurting inside her, filling her, completing her until she collapsed, boneless in his arms.

"Mine," he growled breathlessly as he fought to breath. "Now that I've taken you Tess, I won't let you go."

"Mm," she smiled tiredly. "Give me a minute and you can take again."

Cole chuckled tiredly, rolled from her and gathered her against his sweat-dampened chest.

"Sleep first," he grunted. "Then I'll dominate you some more."

"Or I could dominate you," she suggested with a smile. "Wake you up tied down. Torture you a little."

He gave her a worried look.

"Don't worry, baby," she imitated his slow, sexy drawl. "You'll love it."

## The End

# *Also by Lora Leigh*

ઝ

A Wish, A Kiss, A Dream (*anthology*)

B.O.B.'s Fall *with Veronica Chadwick*

Bound Hearts 2: Submission

Bound Hearts 3: Seduction

Bound Hearts 4: Wicked Intent

Bound Hearts 5: Sacrifice

Bound Hearts 6: Embraced

Bound Hearts 7: Shameless

Cops & Cowboys

Cowboy & the Captive

Dragon Prime

Ellora's Cavemen: Tales from the Temple I  (*anthology*)

Feline Breeds 1: Tempting the Beast

Feline Breeds 2: The Man Within

Feline Breeds 3: Kiss of Heat

Manaconda (*anthology*)

Men of August 1: Marly's Choice

Men of August 2: Sarah's Seduction

Men of August 3: Heather's Gift

Men of August 4: August Heat

Primal Heat (*anthology*)

Savage Legacy

Sealed With a Wish

Shadowed Legacy

Shameless Embraces

Shattered Legacy

Soul Deep

Submission Seduction
The Twelve Quickies of Christmas Volume 1
Wizard Twins 1: Ménage a Magick
Wizard Twins 2: When Wizards Rule
Wolf Breeds 1: Wolfe's Hope
Wolf Breeds 2: Jacob's Faith
Wolf Breeds 3: Aiden's Charity
Wolf Breeds 4: Elizabeth's Wolf
White Hot Holidays Volume 1

*Also see Lora's mainstream fiction at Cerridwen Press*
*(www.cerridwenpress.com)*

Broken Wings

# About the Author

৪১

Lora Leigh lives in the rolling hills of Kentucky, often found absorbing the ambience of this peaceful setting. She dreams in bright, vivid images of the characters intent on taking over her writing life, and fights a constant battle to put them on the hard drive of her computer before they can disappear as fast as they appeared. Lora's family, and her writing life co-exist, if not in harmony, in relative peace with each other. Surrounded by a menagerie of pets, friends, and a teenage son who keeps her quick wit engaged, Lora's life is filled with joys, aided by her fans whose hearts remind her daily why she writes.

Lora welcomes comments from readers. You can find her website and email address on her author bio page at www.ellorascave.com.

## Tell Us What You Think

We appreciate hearing reader opinions about our books. You can email us at Comments@EllorasCave.com.

# Why an electronic book?

We live in the Information Age—an exciting time in the history of human civilization, in which technology rules supreme and continues to progress in leaps and bounds every minute of every day. For a multitude of reasons, more and more avid literary fans are opting to purchase e-books instead of paper books. The question from those not yet initiated into the world of electronic reading is simply: *Why?*

1. *Price.* An electronic title at Ellora's Cave Publishing and Cerridwen Press runs anywhere from 40% to 75% less than the cover price of the exact same title in paperback format. Why? Basic mathematics and cost. It is less expensive to publish an e-book (no paper and printing, no warehousing and shipping) than it is to publish a paperback, so the savings are passed along to the consumer.

2. *Space.* Running out of room in your house for your books? That is one worry you will never have with electronic books. For a low one-time cost, you can purchase a handheld device specifically designed for e-reading. Many e-readers have large, convenient screens for viewing. Better yet, hundreds of titles can be stored within your new library—on a single microchip. There are a variety of e-readers from different manufacturers. You can also read e-books on your PC or laptop computer. (Please note that Ellora's Cave does not endorse any specific brands.

You can check our websites at www.ellorascave.com or www.cerridwenpress.com for information we make available to new consumers.)

3. *Mobility.* Because your new e-library consists of only a microchip within a small, easily transportable e-reader, your entire cache of books can be taken with you wherever you go.

4. *Personal Viewing Preferences.* Are the words you are currently reading too small? Too large? Too… ANNOYING? Paperback books cannot be modified according to personal preferences, but e-books can.

5. *Instant Gratification.* Is it the middle of the night and all the bookstores near you are closed? Are you tired of waiting days, sometimes weeks, for bookstores to ship the novels you bought? Ellora's Cave Publishing sells instantaneous downloads twenty-four hours a day, seven days a week, every day of the year. Our webstore is never closed. Our e-book delivery system is 100% automated, meaning your order is filled as soon as you pay for it.

Those are a few of the top reasons why electronic books are replacing paperbacks for many avid readers.

As always, Ellora's Cave and Cerridwen Press welcome your questions and comments. We invite you to email us at Comments@ellorascave.com or write to us directly at Ellora's Cave Publishing Inc., 1056 Home Avenue, Akron, OH 44310-3502.

erridwen, the Celtic Goddess of wisdom, was the muse who brought inspiration to storytellers and those in the creative arts. Cerridwen Press encompasses the best and most innovative stories in all genres of today's fiction. Visit our site and discover the newest titles by talented authors who still get inspired - much like the ancient storytellers did, once upon a time.

Cerridwen Press

www.cerridwenpress.com

LaVergne, TN USA
31 August 2010
195341LV00003B/19/P